Regency Rumors

The Sinclair Society Series, Volume 1

Bethany Swafford

Published by Bethany Swafford, 2021.

This is a work of fiction. Similarities to real people, places, or events are entirely coincidental.

REGENCY RUMORS

First edition. September 20, 2021.

Copyright © 2021 Bethany Swafford.

Written by Bethany Swafford.

For my parents and sister

Chapter One

The grim-faced butler who opened the door gave me a stern look and declared, "Applicants for the position ought to go around to the servants' entrance."

Startled, I blinked as I struggled to comprehend what he had just said to me. Position? Servant's entrance?

"I beg your pardon?" I managed to ask as I held out my card. I had written Faircroft's address on the back. "I believe there has been some kind of—"

He interrupted me with a huff, snatching the card from my hand. "Always the same," he muttered, just loud enough for me to hear. He stepped back. "Well, come in already, Miss Nelson. I shall have Mrs. Burnham informed of your arrival."

Maybe it was because I didn't have an escort when I knocked on the door, or perhaps because my appearance wasn't quite up to the standards of current fashion. The walking dress I had selected for the visit was several years old, but I hadn't thought it terribly out of style. I could have made the argument it showed the kind of taste that was respected by the ton.

The timing of my visit could not have been at fault. I had arranged to arrive at the beginning of the visiting hours, but in no way could I have thought it too early.

In any event, whatever was the reason for the series of misunderstandings that followed, my confusion was considerable.

A cold wind encouraged me to enter without arguing. Surely I would be able to clear up the misunderstanding better once I was inside rather than on the doorstep. I had barely squeezed through the doorway when the butler closed the door, missing my shoulder by less than an inch. I flinched away on reflex, and so lost my chance to say anything for he walked away, leaving me standing in the hall.

I breathed out, pulling at the gloves on my hands. This was not how I had expected my visit to go. The worst scenario I had imagined was I would be thrown from the house, and only after I had a chance to explain the reason behind my visit. Being mistaken for a servant? That certainly had not come into my head at any point and put quite a damper on my enthusiasm.

Never before had I been left alone in such a manner, and I found it to be an uncomfortable experience. Was such a situation typical for a person seeking a position? I pondered on that as I turned to take in what I could see of the house.

At the very least, I would have a fascinating tale to relate to Aunt Beth when I returned.

I couldn't be sure how long I was left standing there when I was startled by someone speaking. "This way, Miss," a sulky-faced young woman called out from the staircase. "I'm to take you up to Mrs. Burnham."

Taking a deep breath, I walked over to join her. To my surprise, she sniffed derisively and turned her back on me, her nose in the air. As she climbed the stairs ahead of me, I had serious doubts as to the sanity of the servants in the Burnham household. Such behavior would have resulted in dismissal in any other house, so why was it allowed here?

Holding my tongue on the matter, though, I trailed along behind the rude maid until she reached a closed door on the second level of the house. She flung it open and loudly announced, "Miss Nelson, Mrs. Burnham."

I opened my mouth to correct her on my name, but she just continued on her way down the hallway. Left standing at the open door, I glanced from her retreating back to the room before me. "Well, come in," a woman called. "You're late enough as it is. I don't have all day to spend on this."

It was at this point I felt sorry for any poor woman in search of a position in the house. I stepped into the room, determined to set the matter straight. The mistress of the house sat at the desk in the middle of the library. "Good afternoon, Mrs. Burnham," I said, curtsying.

"Come here, girl," she said, lifting her gaze. "I have calls I intend on making this afternoon. I don't have time for any further dilly-dallying."

"Mrs. Burnham, there has been some mistake," I said, hurrying forward. Though she had met me when I was a young girl, it was clear she didn't recognize me. "You see, I'm—"

"Miss Nelson, I requested you be here an hour ago," Mrs. Burnham interrupted, her stare accusatory. "This delay would naturally be an intolerable strike against you, but as I've had few responses to my advertisement I am willing to be lenient. It is imperative I find a competent lady's maid."

I barely kept my jaw from dropping. She truly believed I was applying to be a lady's maid? "M-Mrs. Burnham, there has been a mistake." This was getting out of hand. "I am Miss—"

"Turn around and let me see your hair," she ordered, cutting me off before I could tell her my name. Would I never get to finish an entire sentence? I didn't move, feeling overwhelmed, and she leaned forward. "You have skill with hairdressing. Excellent. I will admit Eugenia's hair is...difficult, but you should have no problem."

I tried to say something, to object to the whole proceeding, but my voice failed me. "Please pull the cord." She turned her gaze back to the paper in front of her and made a notation with her pen. "Now, Nelson."

"Mrs. Burnham, I need to speak to you about the Sinclair family." Perhaps if she heard my family name, she would recognize me! "You see—"

She barely glanced up. "You worked for the Sinclairs?" she asked, her tone thoughtful though she had interrupted me yet again. She waved her right hand before I could correct her on another misapprehension. "It's hardly ideal, I concur, but I won't say anything if you will not. Please pull the cord."

Yes, I should have tried harder to explain then, but I was reeling from being so off balance. I stepped to the wall and pulled obediently on the cord. "Mrs. Burnham, if I might be able to explain—"

She raised her hand, and I stopped speaking, the manners that had been drilled into me as a child reasserting themselves. The door opened, and the sullen maid reappeared. "Please show Miss Nelson out," Mrs. Burnham requested, keeping her eyes on her papers. She rose to her feet. "I will notify you if you have the position and I will detail the specifics then. Thank you, Miss Nelson. Good day."

My mouth opened to try one last time to explain, but she walked out of the room. I had been dismissed and, apparently, forgotten in an instant. The maid cleared her throat impatiently, her rudeness not extending as far as outright telling me I needed to leave. Feeling numb, I turned and walked out.

I followed the maid back down the steps. At the same time, the butler was escorting a young man up.

When we reached the same step, my eyes met his gaze, and for a brief moment, I felt a vague sense of recognition. But right at that moment, I couldn't say why. There was no indication in his face that he recognized me in return. He gave a respectful nod of acknowledgment, and then we were past each other.

Curiously, I glanced over my shoulder when I reached the bottom of the staircase, but he was already out of sight. Puzzled, I opened my mouth to ask the maid if she knew who he was, but given her attitude, I didn't believe she would give me a response. I pressed my lips closed and hoped I'd be able to solve this puzzle on my own.

In any event, a moment later, I was at the front door. The next thing I knew, I was on the doorstep. The door closed firmly behind me, and I flinched at the force she must have used as the wood made a hard thud at my back. It seemed a fitting conclusion to what had been quite the oddest hour I had ever passed.

"Miss Sinclair?" the elderly driver who worked for Aunt Beth called out to me from where he was waiting by the old-fashioned coach. "Is everything well?"

Glancing over my shoulder at the door behind me, I breathed out. What had just happened? I shook my head and started towards the coach. "Thank you for your concern, Simmons, but all is well," I said as the old man held his hand out to assist me. "You may take me home now."

Another scheme to get to the truth was in order, and I needed time to think what it could be.

"JULIET, WHERE HAVE you been? I have been at my wit's end this past hour! Carter said the coach was gone as well. Please tell me you did not just go call on someone alone."

Aunt Beth's voice was horrified while she declared all of this the moment I stepped into the drawing room. "Very well, I will not tell you any such thing," I said lightly. "There. Has that set you at ease, Aunt?"

She was my mother's aunt, really, my great-aunt. Though her once brown hair was silvery gray, no one at first glance would have ever known she was well into her seventies. Though she acted frail when she wanted to be difficult, I had no doubt she had more energy than most people gave her credit for.

"Indeed, it does not! You've been acting quite strangely these past few days, Juliet." My great-aunt jabbed her needle into her fancy needlework she was doing. She had always been clever with a needle and kept it up even at her age. It was a pastime I had no wish to perform more than was necessary given how often I would prick my finger while sewing. "I wish you would tell me what's wrong. I cannot help if you do not."

"You know why I am upset."

She looked up, a frown on her face. "It is nothing more than a silly rumor," she said, her dark eyes sympathetic. "It will pass. In time. As all such things do."

"Silly rumors do not repeatedly appear in the newspaper." There was more anger in my voice than I intended. I curled my fingers into a fist and took a deep breath. "Everyone must be aware of it. They will talk about it, and it will never die."

A sympathetic expression on her face, Aunt Beth caught my wrist in her hand. "Such anger is not becoming in a young lady like yourself. I know this rumor has unsettled you, but you must try not to think of it. There is nothing you can do to stop it at this point."

Heaving a sigh, I forced my hands to relax. "I don't believe that, my dear aunt. In fact, that is precisely the reason I was not able to keep you company this afternoon. I believe I may have thought of a way to fight back."

"Sit down and tell me what you have been doing." Her expression was both concerned and intrigued. "I asked Carter to find you, but she said you had left in the coach. You know it is frowned upon for a young lady to do such a thing alone."

"Well, I couldn't take Carter, could I?" I sat beside her on the chaise. "She had errands you asked her to do. It was easier to go on my own. I went to see Mrs. Burnham. Her husband was one of papa's business associates."

She breathed a sigh of relief. "I suppose as long as she says nothing of your impetuous impropriety, no bad will come of it."

I couldn't help the laugh that came to my lips. "Oh, I'm certain she will say nothing of me to any of her visitors. It was the most disconcerting and highly entertaining thing that has ever occurred to me. She mistook me for an applicant seeking the position of lady's maid."

"She didn't!"

"She did," I said, emphatically nodding my head. "Every time I tried to explain, I was interrupted. It was one of the most ridiculous situations I had ever been in, Aunt Beth. She dismissed me in a matter of minutes, without listening to a word I tried to say to her, and then sent me away with a promise that she would contact me if I was deemed worthy of the position."

Aunt Beth shook her head. "Only you could get yourself into such a mess," she said, a note of amusement showing in spite of her disapproval. "Though I must question the woman's sensibilities. How could she believe a Sinclair would be reduced to such circumstances as to require the necessity of taking a position as a lady's maid? It's ridiculous."

"She thought my last name was Nelson. She had no idea I was a Sinclair." I frowned as I leaned back. "She knows about the rumor though. I did manage to mention the name of Sinclair when I was attempting to set the matter straight, and she assumed I had worked as a maid for my parents. She assured me she wouldn't hold it against me if I took care not to say a word of it to anyone."

"Horrid woman!"

Laughing, I shook my head. "I wouldn't call her that, Aunt. Perhaps confused, or misled, but not horrid."

"Well, I think she is a tottering giglet!"

Even after five years, I hadn't adjusted to Aunt Beth's habit of resorting to Shakespearean insults at the most random of times. Most of the time, I had no notion what she meant when she did so. 'Tottering', on this occasion, I did know, and it was a bit tame in comparison to some words she'd used in the past.

"Mrs. Burnham is hardly feeble, I assure you." 'Giglet' was beyond my comprehension but I had no doubt it was not a flattering term.

With a huff, Aunt Beth raised her needlework again. "Well, at least you will have no more to do with her. What was it you hoped to accomplish by speaking to this woman?"

"Well, I had hoped she would be sympathetic to my plight. She was acquainted with my mother, you know, and the Burnham family visited on many occasions. I thought if I talked to her about the rumor, perhaps she would be willing to tell others it was simply not true. Once one person speaks up, others would be sure to do the same."

My dear great aunt just shook her head at my answer. "Sometimes I am amazed at how you can still think the best of people after everything that has happened in your life. You cannot know how the family has changed these past five years."

"I believe I am the one who has changed. I am not the happy, naive young lady I once was."

Aunt Beth's head came up. "You cannot mean that, Juliet. You are still quite young."

I breathed a sigh. "Young in age, but not in experience." Her life had been so different from mine I doubt she would truly understand. "Don't mind me, Auntie. It's been a strange day."

For a moment, there was no sound but the crackle of the fire. "I received another letter from your uncle." At the change of subject, I barely held back a groan. "His expedition is going well, and he writes about the artifacts that have been found."

Huffing, I resigned myself to hear more of an archaeological expedition I cared nothing for. "Did he? How fascinating."

THAT COULD HAVE BEEN the end of it. In fact, I expected I would hear nothing more of the matter and had already begun a new strategy to combat the idiotic rumors. But much to my surprise, when the next morning dawned, I discovered I was completely mistaken.

"Good morning, Miss Juliet," Carter said, opening the curtains over the windows. For once, I was awake when my aunt's longtime maid arrived, though I hadn't yet forced myself out of my warm bed. "I have a letter addressed to a Miss Nelson. Miss Beth said it is intended for you."

There was no mistaking the curiosity in her voice. Puzzled and intrigued by the unexpected correspondence, I sat up, and she placed my breakfast tray on my lap. Turning, Carter bustled around the room, as though to show she wasn't at all interested in the letter that sat on the side of the tray.

Opting to ignore my chocolate for the moment, I picked it up and broke the seal. Unfolding the paper, I read the unfamiliar handwriting, my astonishment growing with each word. A startled laugh escaped me, and I shook my head. "My goodness."

"Is there something amusing in your letter, Miss Juliet?" Carter asked, finally giving in to her curiosity.

"I find it very amusing," I admitted, looking up. I held the letter in one hand. "I have had my services as a lady's maid engaged for the sum of twenty-five pounds a year and I am expected to perform the basic duties of a maid. The lady writes as though I would not dream of refusing the position."

"How ridiculous," Carter said with a scoff. She shook her head, somehow missing the humor I saw in the news. "Imagine a young lady such as yourself in service. Juliet Nelson, indeed!"

Having learned what the letter contained, she left satisfied. "Yes. Just imagine it," I said softly, setting the message aside. I poured myself a cup of chocolate and sipped it. My eyes kept straying to the sheet of paper. The details it conveyed spoke volumes about the household.

A true lady's maid would not have made quite so many blunders as I had. Despite being late, acting above my station by going to the front door, and leaving no references—and who knew how many other offenses I was not aware of—I had been offered the position at a very high wage. Either there had been no other responses to Mrs. Burnham's advertisements, or the other applicants had all been genuinely appalling.

Poor Mrs. Burnham would be left where she had begun: with no lady's maid in the middle of the London Season.

What I found most intriguing was Mrs. Burnham had sent the letter to Faircroft House. The only way she could have known to do so was if she'd seen the card I had handed to the butler when I'd arrived. If she'd done so, how had she not also seen the name 'Juliet Sinclair?'

"How odd," I murmured. What reasoning must she have used to justify that?

My thoughts went to the oldest Burnham daughter, the only one I had been acquainted with on any sort of level. Eugenia was a sweet child when I knew her, and I wondered whether her character had changed in the eight years since I had last spent time with her. She would be grown up and having her first Season this year.

"I feel quite ancient," I sighed. I wasn't really, being only three and twenty, but I also wasn't a bright-eyed young woman, thrilled and excited over the events, dinners, and balls that came with the flurry of activity that was known as the London Season. Merely thinking of it was exhausting!

I didn't even realize I had the letter back in my hand until I found myself rereading it. There was the barest glimmer of an idea in the back of my mind, one I knew was probably not the best of plans. "Don't be a fool, Juliet," I told myself. "There's nothing you can do."

I forced myself to set the letter down to finish my repast, but again, found my eyes straying to it. When Carter came back in, I had hardly eaten a bite, and she tutted in disappointment. I didn't take much notice of her disapproval, though. I was on the verge of doing something impulsive and ill-advised. I'd wanted a new plan to investigate the rumors and now I knew what to do.

"Carter," I said slowly. "Can you explain to me in detail everything a lady's maid is required to do?"

Chapter Two

"Juliet, don't be a hasty-witted gudgeon! You'll never succeed! You're not meant for that world!"

The moment I stepped into the kitchen as a servant of the Burnham household, I knew Aunt Beth's protesting warnings were going to be more accurate than I had anticipated. My hands felt clammy inside my gloves, and I could feel my heart pounding in my chest. Nevertheless, I kept my chin up, determined not to allow any trace of nervousness to show.

Not here.

By my side was Mrs. Wilder, the housekeeper. In front of me, it appeared most of the Burnham servants were engaged in their work. All motion had come to a halt as I, the newcomer, became the object of open stares. It was nothing less than what I had been warned to expect, but still, it was unnerving.

"This is Miss Nelson," Mrs. Wilder announced. Her tone, oddly enough, was one of annoyance. "She's the new lady's maid."

Her words and tone of voice made it sound as though some great mistake had been made and I was at fault. Perhaps she was trying to discompose me.

Quite honestly, it was working.

Knowing I had to maintain an outward appearance of calm, I met every pair of eyes that openly stared at me. There were two maids, one of whom looked the epitome of shock. The woman at the oven had her arms crossed and a sullen expression.

In fact, I realized no one in the kitchen seemed at all pleased that I was there. My chin came up ever so slightly before I caught myself. While it wasn't in my job description to make friends with them, I was fairly certain it would make my whole situation slightly more bearable if I were to have at least allies among them.

"I am Wilder, the butler." This came from the tall, thin man who had allowed me into the house before. Ah, Mrs. Wilder's husband. I nodded in acknowledgment, not trusting myself to say anything at this point that wouldn't offend everyone in the room. He continued, "I trust you will serve the Burnham ladies to the best of your abilities."

For some reason, I had the feeling the words 'or else' were meant to be attached to the end of his sentence. I wonder what the 'or else' would have been if he had seen fit to add it. In any event, I met his gaze and held myself with as much dignity as I could muster. This was one of the most important things to do at this point. Or so I had been told.

"I shall endeavor not to fall short of the expectations placed upon me," I said evenly. I couldn't show weakness, and I could not let their dislike affect me. I maintained eye contact with him, even though deep down inside I was quaking in my boots. I'd never been on this side of a butler before. I had always been a member of the family, someone to be respected without question or hesitation.

In a completely different life.

It seemed I had passed the butler's inspection, for he turned away to give something else his undivided attention. Or else he had decided I wasn't worth any more of his time. I really couldn't be sure, but I imagined I would find out eventually.

The footman—and I only knew his position from the livery he was wearing—kept trying to catch my eye, a wide grin on his face. Him, I decided, I would need to keep my distance from. A flirtation with anyone, let alone a footman who thought too much of himself, was nowhere on my list of objectives. I felt my cheeks flushing red as I thought of it.

Forcing that thought away and barely keeping back a shudder of disgust, I glanced at the only face that held even a hint of kindness, one that belonged to the kitchen maid. The small, frail girl with big eyes tilted her head, studying me with open curiosity.

This wasn't the entire staff in the house. I knew the grooms would be out in the stable, though I would hopefully not need to cross paths with any of them. And Mr. Burnham's valet would be somewhere in the house, going about his duties for his master. Overall, it seemed like an average sized household for a well-bred and genteel family like the Burnhams.

In fact, it wasn't much different from the kind of household I had known as a child. No. I couldn't think about Faircroft or Westwood Park. It would only lead to homesickness and grief which would get me nowhere.

"Your room will be this way, Miss Nelson," Mrs. Wilder said, reclaiming my attention. She'd moved back to the doorway without me realizing it. I had allowed myself to get too distracted, trying not to think about my past. "I'm only going to show you once, so you best pay attention now."

I had known I wasn't going to be well-liked. I'd been warned over and over it was going to be like this. It would be the height of folly to take such actions and words personally. And yet, it felt highly personal. These people didn't know me, and they were judging me?

The irony was obvious. Where else had I known of one group of people judging someone by their actions or appearance?

Before I could follow that thought through, though, we passed a junction where the servants' areas connected with the main house. I glanced that way and spotted two men at the end of the hallway. The older man with graying hair I realized must be Mr. Burnham. However, there was something about the second, younger man that seemed familiar to me for some reason.

Several steps past the doorway, my breath caught in my throat. He was the same man I had passed after my interview with Mrs. Burnham. And he looked familiar because I did, in fact, know him! From over five years previous! "Mr. Harper," I breathed out, my steps hesitating for only a moment.

What was he doing here? From what little I knew of him, nothing had told me Oswyn Harper, a man who had been one of my brother's closest friends, had any connection with the Burnham family. If he recognized me, I was done for!

My initial panic subsided. He hadn't known me before. There was hope our paths wouldn't cross and he wouldn't be reminded of who I really was.

"Did you say something, Miss Nelson?" Mrs. Wilder asked over her shoulder, catching my attention. We were now approaching the bottom of a narrow staircase.

"No, Mrs. Wilder," I lied, struggling to keep a subservient tone to my voice. After a moment, she seemed to accept my words and started up the steps.

The whole situation was not going as smoothly as I had hoped it would. There had been nothing even remotely smooth about my entrance into the household. I was going to have to keep a stricter watch on my tongue. I'd thought I knew what it meant to keep myself in check, but I was a mere novice at the act.

As I followed my escort through the narrow hallway, I shook my head. I couldn't allow myself to be so sensitive. I had a job to do now, and I had to concentrate my energy on that. Otherwise, this whole charade would have been for nothing.

We reached the very top of the house, yet another unusual place for me to be in. Mrs. Wilder opened the first door to my right and then stepped aside. "This will be where you sleep as long as you remain in this household," she said, barely glancing over her shoulder. "However long that may be."

If all of the household servants acted in this same manner all the time, I couldn't be surprised a new lady's maid hadn't lasted more than a month here. I wasn't about to let myself be scared away, though, and I put on a calm smile. Nothing annoyed people more than the appearance that what they said or did wasn't having the effect they expected.

"Thank you, Mrs. Wilder," I said to the housekeeper. I, for one, was determined to display the manners I had been raised with. "I am certain my days here will be most instructive."

She sniffed again and continued down the hallway, presumably to inspect the other rooms. I stepped into what would be my private area for the duration of my time in the Burnham household. My little trunk had already been placed on the floor by the bed. Without even really thinking about it, my fingers untied the ribbons of my bonnet, and I removed it from my head.

"Well, here I am, for better or for worse," I said aloud. I turned in a slow circle to take in the whole room. Besides the narrow bed, there was a small washstand at the corner with a straight back chair right next to it. A window devoid of any covering allowed the outside light in.

"Well, that will be the first thing I change," I said, eyeing the open view with dislike. While I knew it was unlikely anyone would ever be able to look in, I did not like the thought there was no way to block it off.

Setting my bonnet on the bed, I knelt by my trunk. I ran my hands over it, remembering how I had spent so much care and time in packing everything in. Had it only been one day since I'd done so?

How Aunt Beth had fussed over my going! Up until the moment I climbed into the hackney carriage, she had pleaded with me to stop and think about what I was doing. More than a few Shakespearean insults had left her lips.

Shaking my head, I pushed the thought of her sad, teary eyes out of my mind. I had to keep myself busy, or homesickness would be sure to make me cry. Seeing a face from the past had already upset my peace of mind.

I sincerely hoped there was a reasonable explanation for Oswyn Harper being in the house, and that he wouldn't be back anytime soon. Not that a lady's maid would cross paths with a guest, but unexpected things happen, more often than not. I couldn't afford to get exposed so early into my mission.

Setting myself to the task of making the bare space my own with what I had, I opened my trunk and reached in to pull out my belongings. The goal was that, once I had my things arranged, I would begin to feel more at home. My aunt's words echoed in my mind; her warnings of failure and disaster. "I will succeed," I whispered with as much determination as I could muster up. "I have to."

I'D JUST PULLED THE last item out of the trunk–the one book I'd allowed myself for entertainment–when there was a sharp rap on the door and the squeak of the door opening. Looking over my shoulder, I saw the sullen maid standing there. "Yes?" I asked, raising an eyebrow. The demeanor I'd seen before was her normal disposition. "Did I give you leave to enter?"

"Mrs. Burnham has requested your presence in her dressing room," the maid announced, ignoring my question. "I'm to take you there now."

What? Now? I wasn't to begin my duties until morning. But, what could I do? Refuse and be dismissed without even having a chance to prove myself? That was entirely out of the question. My hands were, figuratively speaking, tied.

"Of course," I said, pushing myself to my feet. I was now at the mercy of my mistress' bidding. With swift fingers, I unbuttoned my pelisse and after I'd shrugged it off, I left it lying on the bed alongside my bonnet. "Let us not waste any time."

An almost sneer crossed the girl's face, making what would have been a sweet countenance ugly. I was unable to keep my eyes from widening in surprise. This was going well beyond the disdain I'd been told to expect, and the disagreeableness I had seen earlier.

It was outright hatred.

No one had ever hated me before. There were, as is common enough, people I did not get on with and some I was indifferent to at best. And I know there were a few who did not care for my company. Sarah Weston was a name that came to mind on that account! But it was never hatred; more of an agreed avoidance.

Avoidance would not be possible in this case.

"This way if you're coming, Miss Nelson," the maid said, a distinct note of insolence in her voice. She turned her back on me and began walking. "Some of us have work to do at this time of the day."

Pursing my lips, I walked out to the hallway. I made sure to close the door firmly behind me. Why was she acting in this manner? It made no sense. I had done nothing to her, and we had barely even met. I pushed it to the back of my mind to consider later when I had more time to do so thoroughly.

"What is your name, girl?" I asked as I followed her down to the family's section of the house. Perhaps the more I became familiar with her, the less her hatred would become? A naive hope, to be sure, but one I had to cling to. I disliked division and conflict, so any attempt on my part to fix the situation would be well worth the effort.

She hesitated. "Mary, Miss Nelson."

Politeness, at least, and that was the last word I heard out of her. However, it was a start. She paused in front of the door and glanced over her shoulder at me. She nodded toward the door and then continued on her way. I watched until she vanished from sight and shook my head.

Taking a deep breath, I smoothed my dark gray dress and tried to convince myself there was no reason to be nervous about the meeting ahead of me. By all rights, the interview should have been the most nerve-wracking part of it all. I grasped the doorknob and pushed the door open. I stepped in and was immediately overwhelmed with pink.

The walls were pink, the paintings were mostly pink, and the curtains were lacy pink. The rugs on the floor were a darker shade, but pink nonetheless.

It was almost nauseating how pink it was in that small space. I had no words, and I believe I stood in the doorway for nearly a minute, just staring at the room. And then I finally saw my employer, blending in because she was wearing—what else?—pink.

"Oh, there you are, Nelson," Mrs. Burnham exclaimed, looking up. She was reclining on the chaise longue in the middle of the room. Thankfully she didn't seem to notice my lack of propriety in standing in the doorway. "I'm so glad you have finally come. There are just so many things that need to be done before the dinner tomorrow night."

A young lady was sitting on a stool next to the lounge, a book on her lap, and she lifted her head to look at me. Instantly, I recognized Eugenia Burnham, part of the reason I had chosen to come to the house. I took a moment to study her.

She was a pretty enough girl. Her eyes were her best feature, I decided. They were a light blue and held an intelligence I couldn't help but like. Her hair, unfortunately, seemed to be a tangled mess of curls, though arranged in a presentable manner. And her dress did nothing to show her figure off the best advantage.

If I were to be perfectly honest, pink was not the right color for her. And so many ruffles and frills were not flattering. For anyone.

"Eugenia, this is the new lady's maid I told you about," Mrs. Burnham said, putting her hand on her daughter's arm. There was an affectionate tone to the woman's voice I had quite honestly not expected to hear. "I tried to convince your father we needed a French maid. Perhaps people will think she is one if we call her Julie? Julie sounds almost French, does it not?"

My jaw clenched at the indignity of being talked about as if I were not in the room. "Mama, I think all we should worry about is whether she is going to stay or not," Eugenia responded, studying me in return. "I thought Papa was going to consider Mary for the position."

Oh. That certainly cleared up my confusion. I should have guessed the root of Mary's animosity towards me. It was no secret that for a maid, advancing to the position of lady's maid was an important step. If I had been in her shoes, how would I have viewed an interloper coming into the house and taking on the position I had aspired to take on?

I would have been incensed. No wonder she had been so hateful!

"Mary hasn't the experience to take on the position," Mrs. Burnham explained, her tone dismissive. She leaned back and closed her eyes. "Perhaps, given time, she will become useful. Right now, though, we need you looking your very best, Eugenia. You know how important it is for the family."

It was as though they had completely forgotten about my presence and I had no idea whether that was good or bad. A servant was supposed to be invisible until they were wanted, but I had been called here so there must have been a reason.

Eugenia shook her head, closing the book she had in her lap. "It's not fair to put all the family's hopes on me, Mama," she protested. "You expect too much from me. I am not the kind of girl that will make the brilliant match that all society will talk of. You know that."

I couldn't help but feel sympathy when I heard her say those words. I remembered feeling doubt and concern that I was not the type of girl young men would be interested when I had first faced the London Season. Brilliant, or at least good, marriages were expected of all well-bred young ladies. To fail was the ultimate disgrace, especially when so much was expected.

But I couldn't express my sympathy. I cleared my throat softly, and they both turned towards me with no little surprise on their faces. "Was there something specific you wanted me to do, ma'am?" I asked. If they said too much and then realized I was there, it could not possibly go well for my future in the household.

"Oh, yes," Mrs. Burnham exclaimed, her tone surprised. Perhaps she had forgotten about me. She waved a hand towards the wardrobe. "Many rips and tears must be seen to as soon as possible. It's been so difficult finding a reliable maid, you understand."

So she had said. More than once. Bobbing a slight curtsy, I went to the wardrobe and began to sift through the mess. There was no care in the way the dresses had been put away, and therefore the wrinkles, stains and, as Mrs. Burnham said, tears in the fabric were horrific.

It was going to take days to repair the damage done if it was even possible at all!

As I got to work assessing which could be salvaged and which garments would have to be given up, I kept my ears open. To my disappointment, Eugenia and her mother only spoke of society happenings; where they were going, who would be there, the latest scandal.

All of a sudden there was the sound of distant shouting. Mrs. Burnham heaved a sigh. "Eugenia, go see what your sisters are quarreling about this time, for I haven't the patience to deal with them," she said, a weariness in her voice that hadn't been there before. "You may take some of the gowns with you, Nelson, and work on them this evening."

"Yes, ma'am," I responded, selecting several I thought had a chance at survival. I could only be grateful she had decided not to refer to me as Julie. No one had called me Julie since...

No. I wasn't going to think about him.

Carefully arranging the gowns on my arm, I waited until Eugenia had hurried out of the room. I needed as much information as I could get. "Miss Burnham is in her first season?" I asked.

There was nothing that would make a mother talk more than asking after her children. If she was a fond mother, that is. "Oh, yes. She's going to be a diamond of the first water, I am certain of it!" Mrs. Burnham exclaimed. "At least, until my other girls become of age to join society."

I had yet to meet the two younger Burnham girls, and I barely remembered them from those times the family had visited. From the shouting, though, I could imagine they were not the well-behaved young ladies they ought to be. "Will there be anything else, ma'am?"

"Oh, no," Mrs. Burnham said, complacently. "Your duties do not begin until tomorrow, as we agreed. What a question, Nelson!"

Then, why in the name of sanity was I in her dressing room with an armful of her…I forced down my annoyance and put on a smile. "Yes, of course. I will bid you good afternoon then."

She waved a hand, in what I was sure must be a habit as often as I'd seen her use it. I slipped out of the room and breathed a sigh. There were still raised voices coming from further down the hallway. Carrying what would be my work for the rest of the day, I hurried back the way I had come.

Nothing seemed to have changed in my room while I had been away. I'd half expected to return to find some bit of mischief done by the others.

Settling into the stiff-backed chair, I pulled out my sewing kit, hoping my meager skills would be up to the task ahead of me. Before I had even begun, there was a knock on my door. "Yes?" I called, my focus on threading the needle in my hand. "You may enter."

There was a slight creak as the door opened. "Juliet Sinclair, just what do you think you are doing?"

Chapter Three

I felt a surge of panic at hearing my real name being spoken in such a stern way. But when I lifted my head, my shock faded into surprise. A smile spread across my face as I recognized the woman who stood in the doorway. "Miss Graham!" I exclaimed, feeling a rush of fondness and relief at seeing a familiar, kind face. I surged to my feet. "How lovely it is to see you again! I didn't know you were employed here!"

Stepping inside, Miss Graham closed the door. Her hair had grown grayer since the last time I had seen her, but the serious expression on her face…oh, I remembered that look all too well.

"Juliet Sinclair, you have not answered my question," she pointed out, ignoring my enthusiasm. And there was that tone I'd heard so many times when I got into mischief as a child. It made me smile when it had caused me to quake in my shoes when I'd been younger. "I thought I must have been mistaken when I saw you earlier."

How well I remembered that stern tone of voice! When had she seen me? "At the moment, I am going to try to save this poor gown." I held a rose pink monstrosity of fabric and lace in my hand. "I'm not entirely certain it is worth the effort, but I must try what I can and hope for the best."

"You know very well that is not what I was asking about," Miss Graham said sharply. She took a seat on the edge of my bed, not waiting for me to invite her to sit. "What are you doing here, in this house, this room? As a lady's maid? You are above this kind of work!"

Sighing, I sank back onto my char. Securing the needle into the fabric, I allowed the dress to fall into my lap. "It was unexpected, and I don't intend for it to be a permanent position. I knew Eugenia needed help to face her first Season, so here I am. As my mother always said, if you can help someone, you should."

"I doubt your mother meant you were to forsake your rank and privileges to serve another family. You cannot have fallen so far from society this is necessary for your survival."

"But I am not forsaking anything, Miss Graham! It happened quite by chance. All Eugenia needs is a good lady's maid to help her show herself to the best advantage. How can I not want to lend my aid to her? I was so fond of her when we were children together."

"Yes, it's true a good lady's maid would do wonders for her," Miss Graham said reluctantly. "Are you so prideful as to think you are the only one who can help her?"

"Certainly not!" I was not so egotistical to believe that! "But I have the advantage of having been in society. I know what she needs, and now I know how to give it to her."

Reaching over, Miss Graham took my hands into hers and squeezed them. "If someone were to discover what you have done, you would be ruined. What you are attempting is pure folly."

"It may be." I pulled my hands free of her grasp. "But Eugenia deserves every chance to be happy. What sort of person would I be if I did not do all I could to help her?"

Miss Graham frowned at me. "Are you so miserable, Juliet, you feel you must help someone else to be so because you are not? Why would you run away so foolishly? Have not your family been kind to you these past five years?"

"I am not running away, and my aunt has been nothing but kindness!" I exclaimed, appalled she would think I had been neglected. "I was not...am not unhappy, Miss Graham. Please believe me when I say that. I wish to help Eugenia as much as I possibly can. And this was the only way I could think to do so."

My former governess tilted her head. "But, surely insufficient time has passed for Mrs. Burnham and Eugenia not to recognize Miss Juliet Sinclair."

"Actually, there has," I said with more confidence than I would have had if she had said such a thing an hour earlier. "We first met Eugenia ten years ago. They visited Faircroft for a fortnight, and it was my task to keep Eugenia entertained. They came three years in a row. Seven years has brought about a great deal of change for me. Mrs. Burnham has already failed to recognize me after two face to face meetings."

Thinking of the exact changes would only serve to break my heart, so I chose to focus on the memories of the Burnhams' visits to my family's estate.

Those perfect summer days were some of my fondest memories. Eugenia and I had been the only girls in the house. We'd managed to sneak away from our governesses and run to the pond to throw stones. We spent hours that day just running free in the sunshine. But it was when Jonathan and his friends,

Oswyn Harper being one of them, joined in on our games that the real fun had begun.

Just thinking of that day brought a mix of happiness and grief to my heart. I shook my head. "But you needn't worry. Eugenia was just a child then, and she did not recognize me when I was in front of her no more than an hour ago. I doubt she will realize her mother's new lady's maid is the teenage girl who played with her during those few summers."

From the way my former governess' face twisted with horror, I could see my words did not reassure her.

"What else is there?"

The question was not one I had been expecting. "What do you mean 'what else is there'? Miss Graham, I have explained—"

"You have a kind streak, Juliet. I know. It's tumbled you into many scrapes as I recall," Miss Graham said, slowly and deliberately. At that moment, I remembered quite clearly why she'd sometimes terrified me when she'd been in charge of my education. "But this is extreme, even for you. So what else are you not telling me? Why have you changed your name and taken this position?"

Sighing, I pulled my hands free. "It's...it's personal."

"I am more than willing to go to Mr. Burnham and tell him you are here," Miss Graham said. I felt my eyes widen. "He's a kind man. I am certain he would not allow the scandal to touch you, but you would be sent back to your uncle. Is that what you want me to do?"

Stunned by the threat, I considered her words. While she was more than likely correct about how Mr. Burnham would react, my uncle's reaction would not be so positive. He would undoubtedly remove me from Aunt Beth's care and find some even more remote relation to hide me away with.

My only hope was to convince Miss Graham my intentions were good. When I met her waiting gaze, I was not encouraged by the expression I saw there. I felt caught in the horns of a dilemma, as the saying goes. "If I tell you, you cannot threaten to reveal me in any way."

Miss Graham's eyes narrowed, and she hesitated. "On the condition I am allowed to reveal you if I think whatever you are doing is dangerous in any possible way," she said after several moments of consideration. "It is the only way I can agree to your terms."

I was reminded of the times we had played chess together, both of us seeking the best advantage. That I had lost to her more often than I had come out the victor was not encouraging. "I can accept that." I took a deep breath. "You remember my father came to London on business that-that last journey he and Mama took?"

If anything, my words made the governess' eyes soften. "I remember."

How could either of us have forgotten that time? "I discovered Mr. Burnham was the man my father met with. I know not why they met or what business they discussed. But it was here, in this house, that my father visited that day."

"What of it?"

Her question made me frown. "You honestly haven't heard?" I had thought by now all would know the terrible rumors that had been circulating London. "They are saying my father and Jonathan were traitors; that they were working for the

French and passed on sensitive documents they acquired and thus prolonged the war."

Gasping, Miss Graham stared at me. "No! You must be mistaken! The Sinclair name has always been a respected one. No one could believe such an obvious fabrication!"

Swallowing hard, I shook my head. "I first learned of it when I read such a comment in The Times. You must understand I cannot allow my family to be slandered so. I'm hoping, somehow, to convince Mr. Burnham to speak up in defense of my father."

"Could you not have made the request as yourself? Why the need for this complicated masquerade?"

Ah, now we reached the point of my tale she was very much not going to like. "I tried," I said, my tone more defensive than I liked. I took a deep breath and exhaled slowly. When I continued, my voice was calmer. "I sent him a letter, requesting a meeting, but I heard nothing in reply. You know I do not go out in society, so I would never meet him face to face."

Frustration showed on my old governess' face. I continued with my explanation. "I then attempted to visit Mrs. Burnham. Only I was mistaken for an applicant for this position, and I could not explain myself. I never imagined I would actually be offered it! But when I was…I thought maybe this was the way I could stop the rumors. I-I could think of nothing else!"

"Why did you not ask for your uncle's help? Surely, he would care about the family reputation."

I shook my head, feeling bitterness rising. "My uncle is off on his archeological expedition," I explained, fighting to keep my tone even. "And even if he wasn't, he detested my father. He would not have a care for how the Sinclair name is viewed. No doubt he would even believe it himself."

"He should care," Miss Graham said, her eyes flashing with anger. "You will have no chance at making a match with this silly rumor being spoken of in society! Has he no intention of seeing your future settled?"

As though I had any prospects now, being an almost penniless orphan! My father's estate had been entailed, and thus had gone to a distant cousin I had never met. I had a small inheritance from my grandmother, but as it was a mere three hundred pounds, it wasn't going to attract any suitors. That, coupled with an uncle who had no inclination to assist in finding me a husband, made it clear wedded bliss was not in my future.

"Miss Graham, you must let me see this through." I pushed away the thoughts of self-pity I had wallowed in all too often. "I have considered every other course of action. You must see that."

"But what can you do as a lady's maid? Why not, instead, act as a companion? It is an acceptable position for someone of your breeding. As a friend of the family, it would be natural for you to do so."

Well, she wasn't threatening to expose me anymore, so it was progress. "There is a level of confidence between a lady's maid and her employer that is unlike any other," I explained. There was doubt in Miss Graham's eyes. "And a lady's maid was needed here. Not a companion. I can speak to Mrs. Burnham, and she will repeat it to her husband. It's improbable, I know, but...it is what it is."

Sitting back, Miss Graham was quiet for what seemed like an eternity. Nervously, I fingered the thread I'd been preparing to work with. I wanted to say something but knew to do so would be counterproductive. "I hate seeing you like this, Juliet," she finally said in the quietest tone I'd ever heard her use. "This is not the kind of life you were ever supposed to know."

She wasn't entirely wrong about that. I nodded to show my understanding. "I know," was all I could think to say.

"You had such good prospects!" she said. I felt a knot of dread form in my throat. "I remember young Mr. Bladen showing you a great deal of attention. I was so certain he would offer for you. You would have had a good life with him; the kind of life you were raised to have."

I closed my eyes at the name. Henry. "I would rather not talk about him, Miss Graham." I had already dredged up far too many bad memories, and I felt as though my heart would break. "It is all in the past and done with."

"He didn't even write to you? After...everything?"

"No, he did not," I said a great deal too sharply. I regretted my tone the moment the words left my lips. It was not her fault the man I thought had loved me had abandoned me the moment he learned I had nothing. She and I hadn't been close enough for any correspondence after my uncle dismissed her.

How could I have loved a strict woman, who believed affection was reserved for children? Miss Graham had exacted excellence in everything, and failure to live up to her standards meant scolding after scolding. Nothing I did was ever good enough; she always said I should have done better.

In any event, she wouldn't have known what had happened after my parents' death. And the name Henry Bladen was not one I wished to hear.

"Forgive me, Miss Graham. I must return to my mending. If you are going to expose me, then please do so and save me the trouble of beginning."

She sighed and got to her feet. "I suppose I should make sure Daphne and Calliope aren't attempting to kill each other again," she decided in an offhand manner. She reached out and put her hand on my shoulder. "I will do everything I can to help you, Juliet, if only to get you back to where you belong."

"I appreciate that," I said, a relieved smile coming to my lips. It was the best I could have hoped for. "I am as anxious as you are that I return to my life as soon as possible."

Miss Graham raised an eyebrow, and she slowly shook her head. "I know how easily you can become bored. I don't think you are in any hurry to return to the normalcy of living with your great aunt and the dullness of an unchanging routine."

I opened my mouth to deny it, but I could not force out a lie neither of us would believe. "Watch yourself, Juliet," she said, putting her hand on the doorknob. "You have put yourself in a difficult position, one that calls for humility. That was never one of your strong points. And pray no one who is personally acquainted with you comes to visit."

"I know," was all I could say. While I felt the compulsion to tell her I had already seen someone I knew, I had the feeling she would change her mind about keeping my secret, and I would be finished.

With a nod of her head, Miss Graham turned and walked out of the room. I heaved a sigh of relief. I hadn't expected to be faced with my former governess, and her presence changed everything I had planned. Though I loved Miss Graham dearly from when she'd taught me, she was entirely too strict about keeping to one's specific place in society. From now on, I knew she would keep an eye on me and what I did. Most definitely not a good thing.

In all honesty, though, she'd taken the news better than I could have expected. But, she also didn't ask the question I thought would come once she knew my main reason for being there; the question I thought was the most important one to ask.

Why, after five years, were people suddenly saying my father and brother had been traitors?

The accusation had sprung from nowhere. I first learned of it when I sat down to peruse the newspapers that were still delivered to the house for my uncle. It had been in a small paragraph, in an article that spoke about the war with Napoleon.

The comment had been vague enough not to be slander, but there was no question to whom it referred. Even now, so many weeks since I had seen it, I knew it by heart:

'Far be it for anyone to speak ill of the dead, but a traitor is a traitor even if they have been dead five years. Father and son left this world soon enough to avoid exposure, but it should never be forgotten the name of S— caused this war to drag on.'

The words left me in shock. Who would dare say such things? My family had done nothing to deserve such an accusation! Neither my father nor my brother had been involved in the war. Not in the actual fighting or the politics waged within the government.

It made absolutely no sense whatsoever to wait five years to dredge up such a strong accusation. Why even bother unless it was for some malicious reason? Or perhaps blame needed to be apportioned and my family provided convenient scapegoats?

Whatever the reason, I was determined to get to the bottom of it. I owed it to my family to clear our name of all suspicion.

But first, I had a dress to repair. I regarded the fabric with the greatest dislike a person can have for an inanimate object. How many times had Miss Graham insisted fine stitching would serve a lady well in life? And she hadn't even noticed I was doing the task!

With a sigh, I settled in for what could only be a dull and tedious evening.

AFTER SEVERAL HOURS, my hands and eyes could not take the strain any longer. Sighing, I set aside my work and stood. I had not accomplished as much as I would have liked, but the dress was proving challenging to salvage with so many tiny tears and rips in the fabric. How had Mrs. Burnham allowed her wardrobe to deteriorate into such a state?

I wondered what she could have left to wear to the engagements she must have attended while looking for a new lady's maid, but then I remembered the large number of gowns that had been crushed together. For every ruined dress, she merely ordered a new one to take its place.

Shaking my head, I stretched my stiff and sore muscles as I got to my feet. I wasn't in the habit of sitting in one position for such a long time. I reached my hand up and curled my finger around the gold chain hung around my neck. A gentle tug was all it took to bring it up from where it was kept hidden beneath the fabric of my dress, and the pocket watch that I kept secured on the chain was in my hand.

What should have been, had always been intended to be, passed onto my brother was now mine. It had been my father's watch, and it was the one tangible thing I had to remember him by. He had always carried it and after the accident...I don't even remember who had placed it in the palm of my hand and curled my fingers around it. Now, I never went anywhere without it.

I ran my thumb over the glass as I read the time. The Burnhams would be having supper at this time, which left me with the perfect opportunity to explore some of the house and learn my way around.

Allowing the watch to slide back out of sight, I snatched up my shawl from where I had let it rest on the bed. Slinging the soft fabric around my shoulders, I walked to the door. All was quiet in the hallway as I made my way to the staircase. I wasn't often in the attic of any house, so it was strange seeing the lack of the things I would typically associate with a hallway: carpets, paintings, vases of flowers, or any decoration.

The steps creaked as I went down them. That, oddly enough, was a sound I was used to hearing. Faircroft was a house where many generations had lived, and Aunt Beth had always said each squeak and creak was the house's way of speaking to us. Like an old woman fussing at the change happening around her.

Thinking of that reminded me of a task I hadn't yet completed. Aunt Beth was going to be so worried. I had promised I would send her a note so she would know I had arrived safely and I hadn't been tragically kidnapped in the short distance from Faircroft to the Burnham's house.

Determining to write the short message before I went to sleep, I entered the family's part of the house, and the difference was apparent immediately. The floors were covered with soft carpets, and the walls were papered in a light floral design. I started along the hallway, counting doors as I went. I was working up the courage to enter one of them.

"Are you lost, girl?"

I spun around at the deep voice. A tall, well-built man in a modest black suit was now standing in the doorway of one of the rooms I had just passed. Mr. Burnham's valet. I knew I ought to keep my head down and get back to my room before I stirred up trouble or brought undue attention to myself, but I couldn't bring myself to lower my gaze.

"I am not," I said, my tone as polite as I could manage. "My name is Miss Nelson. I am the new lady's maid."

The man raised an eyebrow. "Julie Nelson, are you? Well, well." he said, his tone slightly curious. There was a pause, just long enough to make me nervous. "Ah, I see I need to introduce myself. I am Bridge, the master's valet. I was given to understand the new lady's maid would be arriving tomorrow."

With a nod and a brief curtsy, I said, "I am to begin my work tomorrow. However, I arrived today. I am acquainting myself with the house so I may complete my tasks without unnecessary delay tomorrow morning."

We stared at each other for a moment longer before he inclined his head. "Enjoy your last free evening, Miss Nelson," he said and then turned back into the room. The door closed behind him a moment later.

Well, at least one person in the household staff seemed to accept my presence with no ill will. But why had he looked so surprised when I introduced myself if he had been told I was to arrive?

Left once again to my own devices, I completed my count of the doors. As I now knew where the master and mistress' bedchambers were, I could begin guessing at the other bedrooms and Eugenia's room. I would need to know each location if there happened to be any guests I would have to look after while I was in service in the house.

There were three guest rooms in total, one decorated in greens, another in pale yellows, and the last in a calming blue. I didn't imagine the Burnhams ever had many overnight guests, but their family would come for visits throughout the year. I sincerely hoped the duration of my stay would be without the added responsibility of looking after any guests!

I'd just finished my evaluation of the floor and committed it to memory when I heard someone clearing their throat behind me. I spun around for the second time, mentally growling at being interrupted in my self-appointed task yet again. My breath caught in my throat, and I made a squeaky sound of surprise.

"I didn't mean to startle you," Oswyn Harper said, holding his hands up. "Please forgive me!"

"Well, you did!" left my mouth before I could stop it. My tone was defensive and accusing. My hand flew up to my mouth.

A bemused frown appeared on the man's face. "Excuse me?"

Drat my tongue and its ability to not listen to my brain! "Pardon me?" Forcing a confused, innocent tone into my voice, I allowed my hand to drop. "Do you require assistance, sir?"

Mr. Harper paused and blinked. "Who are you?" he asked. His frown returned. "Wait. You look familiar. Have we met?"

I had hoped the shadows in the hallway would keep my features hidden. I tried to think quickly. He was not speaking to me in the manner a gentleman would with a lady, which was a blessing. I could work with that.

"I am Nelson, Mrs. Burnham's new lady's maid," I said, putting as much professionalism into my voice as I could. He gave a start as though he was not expecting those words to come out of my mouth. "You may recall we passed each other on the staircase a week ago."

There was a pause. "I see," he said slowly.

An awkward silence formed, as though he did not know what to do next. I barely kept from fidgeting. "Do you require assistance, sir?" I asked again when I could not bear the silence a moment longer.

"No. I merely came up to retrieve a letter I left in my room."

His room? None of the guest rooms I'd been in had shown any sign of being occupied. "Of course, sir," I said, just as slowly as he had spoken. I bobbed a slight curtsy. "I will bid you goodnight then."

"Good evening," he said automatically, still regarding me with puzzlement in his eyes.

The door back to the attic was behind him. My steps were cautious as I went towards him. He took a step to the side, continuing to watch me. I didn't dare look away as I edged around him, keeping as much distance between us without actually pressing myself up against the wall.

Once I was around him, I deliberately turned, though I wanted to be able to keep my eyes on the man for as long as possible. Somehow, I don't think it would have looked natural or innocent if I walked backward for the length of the corridor. I reached the connecting hallway and stepped through.

I made sure to wait a few seconds before peeking through the crack between the slightly ajar door and the doorframe. Mr. Harper entered the Blue Room. Now I was even more confused than I had been before. Had I been careless enough to miss the evidence of someone staying in that bedroom?

A minute passed before Mr. Harper left. He walked down the hallway and stopped at a different door. The one leading into Mr. Burnham's room. I felt a frown crease my forehead as he entered. What was he up to?

The door closed behind him and remained shut. I waited for several minutes, but he didn't come out. The time stretched, fraying my nerves. Getting caught by another servant was the last thing I could have happen. Though I knew it wasn't unusual for servants to spy on their employers, the household here had already shown they didn't trust my presence. Without a doubt they would use this against me if they could!

Breathing out, I pulled the door closed and then rushed to the attic. It was staggering even to consider. I hadn't seen Oswyn Harper in years, and when I do, he's sneaking into rooms he had no right to be in? What was that about?

"Slow down, Juliet." I couldn't know he wasn't supposed to be there. I shook my head as I allowed myself into my room. I was so distracted by my thoughts it took me several seconds to see something significant. "I don't believe this!"

The gown I had been so meticulously repairing lay in tatters on my bed. "No. Nonono!" I snatched it up but didn't have to look close to realize it was beyond saving.

Furious, and on the verge of tears, I threw the pile of shredded silk at the wall and turned my back as it slid down to the floor. However much they disliked me, this was taking things too far. "Much too far," I muttered, brushing at my eyes. I hadn't been out of my room for very long either! Had one of them been watching me?

I was angry, but what could I do about it? Slowly, I sank onto the side of the bed and rubbed the sides of my head with my fingers. I could feel a headache coming on as I tried to calm down. In all honesty, there was nothing that could be done to fix the situation and no one I could tell.

It took several minutes of deep breaths before I finally felt calm enough. I picked up the dress from the floor and tossed it into the scrap basket. At least the other two gowns were untouched. All of my work hadn't been completely undone.

Going to my trunk, I pulled out my precious stack of paper, and the bottle of ink I'd brought with me. I retrieved a quill and glanced around for a flat surface. There was nothing in the room. Carter had never mentioned whether a desk was a common item for a lady's maid to have, but I made a note to request one.

Kneeling down on the floor, I used the seat of my chair as a makeshift desk. I checked the tip of my pen and found it sharp and ready. Dipping the end into the ink, I began my letter in vague terms in case it were to fall into the hands of one of the servants.

Dear Miss Rycroft,
I have arrived in my new household. There was no trouble between here and there, which should relieve you. I am, at this mo-

ment, writing to you from my room. It leaves much to be desired, but I believe I shall become accustomed to it...

Chapter Four

When I forced my eyes open, I couldn't remember where I was or what had awakened me. I was not in my own, bright room at Faircroft, that was for sure. A sharp rap on the door and the almost sullen voice that called through the wood, though, was a quick reminder of my situation.

"Miss Nelson."

"Yes, I'm awake," I called back, my voice hoarse from sleep. I cleared my throat as I propped myself up on my elbows. There was another knock on my door, much rougher than before, and I called out with a stronger voice, "Yes, yes. Thank you. I am awake."

Footsteps faded away, and I let myself fall back onto the hard bed that I'd spent a mostly sleepless night on. I brought my arm over my face with a groan, just thinking of the day I knew I had before me. Two ladies to dress and tidying to be done. Plus an endless pile of mending to do. It was almost enough to make me want to cry for tiredness. And I hadn't even begun!

"Well, lying around in bed will be the fastest way for me to lose my position," I said aloud. Taking a deep breath, I forced myself to my feet. "I can do this."

I'd spent days practicing for this day, under the eye of one of the most scrupulous people I knew. I wasn't about to waste her time or mine.

There was a chill in the air, or it may have been because I was used to a warm fire burning in my own fireplace when I woke up in the morning. It was yet one other thing I had not expected but would have to become accustomed to as long as I was in service. I shivered as I hurried to pull my nightdress off.

Pulling out the gown and accessories that I would wear for the day, I frowned at the stays. The maid should have stayed long enough to lace me up. I made a mental note to have a word with her when she brought me tea and breakfast. I knew very well that if I allowed her, or any of the other servants of lower rank than I, to avoid their duties even once, I would never be able to exert any authority over them during the rest of my stay.

Maintaining the right balance was going to be even more difficult than I initially thought. I had no desire to be an autocratic person, but to be a successful lady's maid I was going to have to be. At least on a small scale.

After I rubbed my arms to get warm, I quickly changed out of my nightgown and slipped into the undergarments. To save a bit of time, I pulled on my stockings and then laced up my sturdy boots. Knowing I must have looked quite the picture, I was glad no one was there to witness it as I was forced to wait.

The door opened behind me, and I spun around. The sullen maid I'd had so many unpleasant dealings with entered with my tea. Finally.

"Set it over there, please." I gestured to the small table in the corner.

As she set the tray down the china rattled, almost as if she were nervous. Frowning, I watched her from my seat on the side of my bed as I wracked my brain, trying to remember her name. As soon as she faced me, she balled her hands into fists. "Will there be anything else, Miss Nelson?" she asked, just the barest hint of insolence in her voice.

Mary. That was it. That was her name. "Yes. Please lace up my stays, Mary," I said, making sure to keep my voice firm. "Also, hot water. See to it, and I may not report your insolence to Mrs. Wilder."

Her chin came up. "That's not my job."

Well, I had been warned of these kinds of challenges to my position. I rose to my feet and took one step towards her. "Which part do you question? Because I believe, Mary, that it is your job to assist me in dressing, and if you ever want to advance, you're going to have to perform your duties without having to be reminded. As to the water, I suggest you take the time to discover who is required to bring it before I decide to report you to the mistress and you lose your position."

For a moment, I thought the girl was going to defy me further, and I held my breath, hoping she wouldn't be so foolish. "Yes, miss," she finally muttered. Mary ducked around me and grabbed the stays. I had to bite back a yelp as she jerked hard. She didn't say a word as she helped pull my gown over my head, and then she was gone.

I sincerely hoped that she would bring me the water I had requested. Mrs. Burnham, if she even listened to my complaint, would merely speak to the housekeeper. Mrs. Wilder hadn't seemed like one who would tolerate any meddling in her affairs, which included the lower servants, and I had my doubts she would dismiss Mary. Especially knowing the family already had a great deal of trouble retaining servants.

If they knew I could not retaliate, the maids would do none of the tasks I asked of them. It would, quite simply, become an impossible nightmare. And I would be unable to do anything, either to help Eugenia with her season or find out what I needed to know.

Shaking my head, I took my time with my tea and toast. After ten minutes, Mary was at my door once more with the hot water, which she poured into the plain wash basin. I sipped my tea, watching her complete the task.

"I expect to have hot water when I rise tomorrow morning," I informed her when she turned towards the door.

She went still for a moment. "Yes, miss," Mary mumbled, her voice ten times as sullen as I had heard the day before. She closed the door as she left and I breathed a sigh of relief.

I had always heard that lady's maids were the most despised among servants, with only the lowliest scullery maids as competition for the title, but I'd never really believed it to be true. I suppose being directly under the mistress of the house, having her confidence, and receiving her cast-off clothing would make for some jealousy from the other maids.

Rather foolishly, I'd thought the camaraderie between servants would make my investigation easier. How was I to get the trust of my now fellow servants? Would they divulge any information if I asked? Or would they be tight-lipped because I was a newcomer and had taken the position one of their own had hoped for?

Sighing, I finished my tea and set the cup on the table. I quickly washed and dried my face, nearly burning my fingers in the almost boiling water. I smoothed the fabric of my gown and faced the door. Perhaps this day had not begun as well as I hoped it would, but it was time for my work to start.

One of the true benefits of being a lady's maid was that I was not required to wake as early as most in the household. Still, as I made my way to the dressing room, the house was quiet. I thought I caught a glimpse of the second maid, the one whose name was unknown to me, scurrying to complete her duties.

As I feared, the dressing room was a chaotic mess. Mrs. Burnham had left her gown from the previous evening on the floor, along with the day dress she'd been wearing when I had been in the room. There were three different shawls, and at least five different pairs of gloves laying on the table, not to mention the slippers and boots on the floor.

Heaving a sigh, I got to work, putting away the two gowns I'd managed to repair the evening before. However much a disaster the room seemed, it was my place to organize and put things away. It was what a lady's maid was required to do.

I could only be grateful that my mother had taught me the value of neatness and to respect not only the clothes I had but also those that had to come after me to maintain the room. I could honestly say that, once I was grown, I had never been guilty of leaving a place in such a deplorable state. I would have been in a great deal of trouble with Mama if I ever had. Even worse, I would have disappointed her.

Disappointing Mama would have broken my heart.

I curled my fingers around a soft shawl and took a deep breath. I did not need to think about Mama or the life I'd had before. If I did so, I knew I would just sit down and cry. Instead,

I forced myself to consider just what I would change to make the dresses more appropriate for my employer.

That line of thought kept me well entertained because there was so much fashionably wrong with the gowns. And it wasn't a matter of personal preference. Mrs. Burnham had a taste for frills and feathers. A few of each could set off a gown beautifully, but the quantity that Mrs. Burnham's dresses had was simply....horrific.

By the time I had the room and wardrobe in some semblance of order, it was time for me to take Miss Eugenia her tea. Immediately after I would have to deliver the same to Mrs. Burnham.

I was proud when I arrived in the kitchen without once taking a wrong turn. Thankfully, the tray was ready. I would not have been surprised if the cook had mysteriously 'forgotten' that it was needed. Perhaps the woman knew she would be the one in trouble if such a thing occurred.

Balancing the tray carefully, I returned upstairs and made my way to Eugenia's room. "Good morning, Miss Burnham," I said as I entered. She had, as I discovered the evening before, a charming room all to herself and there was not even the slightest shade of pink to be seen.

The girl in the bed stirred and pushed herself up. "Oh, Nelson, it's you," she said, rubbing at her eyes. Was that disappointment I heard in her voice? She reached out to accept the tray. "Good morning."

Either she was a light sleeper, or she'd already been awake. I handed her the tray and then strode to the windows. "I hope you slept well," I said, pulling the curtains open without really looking out. I turned to face her.

"I did, thank you." Eugenia leaned back against the bed frame. She flipped her messy braided hair over her shoulder and poured a cup of chocolate. "I was expecting Mary to bring up my breakfast."

Had everyone expected the maid to be promoted to the position? Why had she not been?

"Well, you have me, Miss Burnham, and I hope I don't disappoint you," I said with as sincere a smile as I could manage. "I will leave you to eat, and then I will return to help you dress."

"You can just send Mary up. I know my mother will require all of your attention."

I gritted my teeth. "Of course, Miss Burnham," I said as politely as I could. "I will let Mary know that you require her."

It took all the self-control I could muster to keep from muttering all the way down to the kitchen. The second tray was ready, and I grabbed it. The cook raised an eyebrow but wisely said nothing. On my way up, I collected the correspondence that had arrived for Mrs. Burnham.

Quite honestly, the quiet in the house was almost familiar, and it calmed me down. I always loved mornings and the serenity that often accompanied them.

Breathing out a slow sigh, I accepted the fact that Eugenia would naturally want someone she was familiar with to attend to her, and it was unfair to expect her to trust me immediately. She didn't know me; not as Julie Nelson. It would take time to build trust between us. Fortunately, time was the one thing I had plenty of, and I could make myself patient.

Mrs. Burnham's room was dark, and the air smelled stale when I stepped in. "Good morning, ma'am," I said, forcing a note of cheerfulness into my voice. How well I remembered being pulled from sleep in such a manner not so long ago! "I trust you slept well."

"Hmm?" Mrs. Burnham mumbled something unintelligible in response to my greeting. She rolled over and pulled the covers over her head.

Frowning, I set the tray on the bedside table and pulled out my father's watch to check the time. It was the hour Mrs. Burnham had specified, but she was not awake. For a moment, I hesitated. Did I continue with my tasks, or should I wait?

Remembering how often Carter, Aunt Beth's maid, had insisted on throwing open the curtains and pulling me out of bed at the same time every morning, I headed for the windows. "It's going to be a beautiful day, ma'am," I said as I pulled the curtains open. The fact that it was gray and dull outside gave me pause. "Oh."

Before I could retract or modify my statement, I heard the door squeak open. Spinning on my heel, I watched Mary pour hot water into the wash basin. She didn't glance over at me and was quick to leave. Trying to still the tremble in my hands that gave away my nervousness, I marched over to the stand, straightened the towel there, and made sure it was ready for use.

And then I was left with nothing to do. Mrs. Burnham still hadn't moved, and I had no notion as to what I was to do next. I would be sure to be in trouble if her tea became cold.

"Mrs. Burnham!" I said quickly before I lost my nerve. Again, there was no response from the bed. I took a few steps closer. "Mrs. Burnham. A letter has arrived, franked by Lord Jersey."

She sat up so fast I jumped back in surprise. "Where?" Her demand bore no hint of sleepiness. "Hand it to me right away! Why did you not say anything earlier?"

"Here, ma'am," I responded, picking up the tray from the table where I had left it. I placed it on her lap and gestured to the pile of letters. "I will return to assist you to dress."

She made no reply as she broke the seal on the letter from Lady Jersey, and I quickly left the room. "You only have one first day," I said to myself as I returned to the dressing room next door. I selected a morning gown that I thought would be to Mrs. Burnham's tastes and laid it out.

"I have never met anyone who loved one color so much," I said, running my hand over the pale pink fabric.

Shaking my head, I hurried out. I hadn't forgotten Eugenia's request, and I didn't want to disappoint her. Fortunately, I met Mary on the stairs. "Miss Burnham has requested that you assist her today."

My blunt statement startled her, and she came to a complete stop. "She has?" Mary rubbed the back of her neck even as her eyes brightened. She cleared her throat and forced all emotion off her face. "I will see to her then."

I nodded curtly and stepped aside to allow her to go on. I breathed out as soon as I was alone once more, welcoming the brief time I had to compose myself before returning to Mrs. Burnham's room.

MRS. BURNHAM WAS SITTING up in her bed. "There you are, Julie," she said, setting aside her tray. I held back a sigh at the name, knowing there was no chance of escaping it. She waved a sheet of paper in the air. "This is the most fantastic news! We are to attend Lady Jersey's ball next week!"

"That is good news." I picked up the tray, carrying it away from the bed. It looked as though she hadn't eaten a bite, though the teapot was empty. I set it by the door, to be picked up by one of the maids, before transferring the other, unopened letters to her bedside. "Miss Burnham will be thrilled when she hears the news, I'm sure."

"This is exactly the invitation to propel Eugenia into the right society," Mrs. Burnham said with a pout. A slight frown crossed her face. "How strange that we suddenly receive an invitation now. Who would have arranged this? Perhaps it was Landon! I knew his intentions towards Eugenia were more serious than he let on!"

A choked cough left me before I could stop it, but she paid me no attention. Did she honestly believe a gentleman would make such a grand gesture for a girl he must know very little about? The season had begun only a few weeks previous, though it was possible the Burnham had been acquainted with the gentleman before the season began.

I had guessed that Mrs. Burnham was the kind of woman who desired her daughter to make a stir if they should ever acquire tickets but had never actually made the effort to cultivate an acquaintance with the ladies who ruled over Almack's, the most exclusive assembly rooms in London.

It was, perhaps, good for Eugenia's cause that my mother had been acquainted with several of the patronesses.

Mr. Gerard Landon was a name known to me. He was a well-respected younger son of a country baron. I'd met him briefly when I spent a short time in London nearly six years ago. He had been well-mannered and polite, and I had been eager to further my acquaintance with him.

If he were truly interested in pursuing Eugenia, I was delighted for her.

"Send for Eugenia immediately, Julie," Mrs. Burnham said, turning her attention on me. "She must learn of her good fortune right away!"

"Yes, ma'am," I said promptly. "Shall we get you dressed first?"

Mrs. Burnham lifted her head and scowled. "Certainly not. There's more than enough time before I must be up and about for our callers later on. Fetch Eugenia from the schoolroom this instant, Julie."

The schoolroom? Why was Eugenia in the schoolroom? Stepping back, I nodded. "Right away, Madame." Spinning on my heel, I walked out of the bedroom. I heaved a sigh. I had known that Mrs. Burnham was not of a calm disposition when I had decided to come. I could handle it, though.

At least, that's what I kept trying to convince myself.

As I made my way up to the schoolroom, I took in the house as it was meant to be seen: in the daylight. In general, it seemed to be very tastefully decorated, besides the horrendous pink dressing room. It was the kind of dwelling I would expect any genteel family to spend the London Season in. It was not, as was usually the case, a rented townhouse meant to be inhabited in the spring, but their year-round dwelling.

I had researched the family beforehand, wanting to know as much as I could before I immersed myself into the household. The family was relatively well off, though not as wealthy as they had been in earlier years. While Mr. Burnham owned land in the North, which he had inherited from his father, the funds he gained from the estate were not enough to afford a townhouse.

Mrs. Burnham had brought a great deal of money to her marriage, allowing her husband to employ a steward to run his estate while the family lived in London. But the majority of that money had gone into the upkeep of the London house, or at least that's what the rumor was. Mr. Burnham had some position in the government, but it was unclear what exactly it was.

All of this I had learned from Aunt Beth, who had been eager enough to tell what she knew. I suspect Aunt Beth thought this background supported her opinion that Mrs. Burnham was an unintelligent being.

Feeling a bit tired of the whole affair, I walked towards the schoolroom. Even if I hadn't known where it was, the two voices yelling on the other side of the door in what must have been a competition of some sort would have informed me. I opened the door and slipped inside.

In the middle of the room, Miss Graham was standing in between two young girls. "This kind of behavior is appalling!" She had a hand on each girl's shoulder, clearly trying to keep them apart. "Neither of you shall be walking out today."

"We will!" the older of the two girls—Calliope, I guessed— declared. There was no mistaking the family resemblance between the Burnham girls. They all had the unfortunate curly brown hair that seemed untamable. "I shall ask Mama, and she will say you are to take us! So there! We will go walking."

"No, I will tell Mama!" the second girl exclaimed. Her brown hair was a mess that would have appalled any mother.

Well, any mother who cared to have their children looking presentable at all times. "Just because you are oldest, Calliope, doesn't mean you get to tell Mama everything!"

Miss Graham looked as though she either wanted to pull her hair out or strangle them both. I knew it was a sentiment that I would share if I were required to be in charge of two such unruly children!

"Nelson, does Mama want me?"

I'd been so distracted by the quarreling girls that I had completely missed seeing Eugenia sitting at the window. "Yes, Miss Burnham," I responded as I found myself under the gaze of everyone in the room. "I believe she has news she wishes to impart."

"You're the new maid?" Calliope asked, her tone incredulous. "But Mary said that you were a horrible, ugly—"

"My hair is a mess, Nelson," Daphne interrupted, imperiously. I wasn't sure whether I wanted to know how Calliope would have finished her sentence. Daphne pulled away from Miss Graham and came towards me. Her hair looked as though it had, at some point during the morning, been tied back with a ribbon. I wondered whether it had been Mary's doing, or if Daphne had made an attempt herself. "You must fix it. Immediately."

A deep breath was necessary to remain calm. I could not let her get under my skin. "Miss Daphne, I am not required to fix your hair. I believe you ought to speak to Mary or do so yourself," I said, meeting her gaze. I was satisfied to see her pause in surprise. Not many people must tell her no. "Miss Burnham, your Mother wished to speak to you as soon as possible."

A smile was playing on the oldest Burnham girl's lips as she watched the interchange. How nice to know I amused her. "Yes. I must not keep Mama waiting," she said, standing up. "Calliope, Daphne. Listen to Miss Graham and do your schoolwork. You don't want to be outside today, anyway. It's far too wet."

Both of the younger girls made faces at their older sister's back as soon as she passed them. I caught Miss Graham's eye briefly, and she just shook her head. I lifted one shoulder in a shrug as I turned to escape the room, leaving the governess to her two charges. "I'm going to tell mama that you were disrespectful!" Daphne called after me. "Just you wait! You'll lose your position!"

A dozen different responses came to my head that would have only made it worse. Instead, I said in a polite tone that had always incited a scold from my mother for being on the brink of rudeness, "Certainly, Miss Daphne. Of course, your mother is free at any time you wish to do so. Shall I inform her that you will be coming to speak to her later on?"

My words brought a look of complete shock to the girl's face. Taking a step back, I firmly closed the door behind myself. "You are the strangest lady's maid I have ever met," Eugenia said, staring at me when I turned around.

Somehow, that surprised me. Lady's maids are supposed to be clever, even if they were to keep quiet until their opinion or observation was asked for. "Your mother was most insistent that you come to her now, Miss Burnham," I said gently.

Eyeing me for one more second, Eugenia set off, and I followed a few steps behind her. When we arrived at the correct room, Mrs. Burnham hadn't moved from her bed, and she still held that one letter in her hands. "Eugenia, all is going according to plan!" she exclaimed, on seeing her eldest daughter. "We have been invited to Lady Jersey's ball next week!"

"What?" Eugenia exclaimed, taking a seat at the side of her mother's bed. I busied myself at the dressing table, acquainting myself with the myriads of bottles that stood there. "Are you certain?"

"Here, read for yourself," Mrs. Burnham said, pushing the letter into Eugenia's hands.

To my surprise, Eugenia didn't seem at all pleased as she read the message. "But Mama, who would have done this for us?" she asked when she lifted her head. "We do not know Lady Jersey, and she is not the sort to extend an invitation for no reason at all. I thought you said all of your acquaintances refused to make an introduction."

"Isn't it obvious, my dear? Landon is certainly the one behind it!"

"Mama, he would never have done such a thing," Eugenia said in protest, her cheeks bright red. It was not the light blush of youth that could be so charming. It was almost as though she'd been in the sun for too long. "It would mean that we were practically engaged, and we are not! I've only conversed with him a few times!"

"Of course, perhaps you could do better," Mrs. Burnham remarked, completely ignoring her daughter's words. She took the letter from Eugenia. "There are a few titled men this season who might be on the lookout for a young wife. Any one of them would make an excellent husband for you if we overlook a few youthful indiscretions. And a first son is always more desirable than a second."

"Mama!"

I glanced between them. Every mother wanted a good match for their daughter, a wealthy one if at all possible. I knew that. Everyone knew it to be true. But this was extreme. My eyes returned to Eugenia's face, and I studied her expression. She may have protested Landon's indifference, but I had a feeling that wasn't what her heart said.

She looked as though she had already fallen for the man.

Chapter Five

"Eugenia, your hair looks terrible! Julie, what were you thinking? This will not do at all!"

Flinching, I looked closer at the way Eugenia's hair was arranged. It was simple enough, and I could see no problem with it, beyond the fact it had become more frizzed overnight. "I will see to it immediately," I said, choosing my words carefully. "Miss Burnham requested Mary assist her dressing this morning, therefore I—"

"It is not Mary's job to dress Eugenia; it is yours!" Mrs. Burnham glared at me with obvious disapproval and annoyance as she cut me off mid-sentence. I had not chosen my response carefully enough. "I made this clear when we discussed your duties. Eugenia, you will do well to remember this yourself!"

"But Mary knows all sorts of tricks for working with my hair!" Eugenia protested, looking and sounding genuinely distressed. "I thought it simpler if Nelson was able to focus on you, Mama! She is your maid, after all."

"Well, I am not the one who must attract a husband, am I? You must have a care about your appearance, my dear. Especially now we will be attending Lady Jersey's ball!"

Eugenia flushed that unfortunate red hue once again. "I cannot understand why you will not allow Mary to be my personal lady's maid if you are so concerned with my appearance!" she fired back, her eyes flashing with anger. That was my question too, and I glanced between them. "You will never be satisfied with the results if Nelson must see to us both!"

While she had a valid point, the way Eugenia said it would not go over well with her mother. "Eugenia, enough," Mrs. Burnham ordered. She raised a hand to her head. "It is far too early to be arguing over such trivial matters. I can feel a megrim coming on."

The young lady looked as though she wanted to say more about the matter but did not. "Of course, Mama, I'm sorry to have distressed you. Thank you for telling me the good news. I will join you when we make our calls this afternoon."

She left her mother's bedroom. Shaking my head, I made a mental note to speak to her later and turned to my task. It was tedious work to get Mrs. Burnham dressed. First her stays were too tight and then not tight enough. The dress I had brought out for her was not what she wanted and it took me three more tries to find the correct one. When she was finally dressed and with her hair arranged precisely as she wanted, she went down to the hall to leave with Eugenia for a visit to the shops.

Breathing out a sigh, something I felt I had been doing quite a bit of since I'd stepped foot in the house, I began to straighten the room. I threw open the windows, shivering in the cold wind. Within moments, the room smelled fresher. The wash basin and jug needed cleaning, and a clean towel laid out.

Then, it was back into the dressing room to continue with the repairs needed to the garments. The careless way the dresses had been put away had a great deal to do with the damage done to the fabric, but I couldn't understand why Mrs. Burnham had allowed things to reach this state. Surely whichever maid had been handling these duties before would have taken more care than this.

Or, perhaps it was yet another way to drive me from the position.

While I did not hate needlework, I would hardly have classified it as a favorite activity of mine. Pink, on the other hand, I honestly did detest, and facing so many different shades of the same color at one time was exceedingly repulsive to me. Of all the things I had imagined I would dislike about the position, nothing compared to this.

I was entirely occupied with my mending until my growling stomach forced me to take a brief break and go in search of sustenance. Going into the kitchen first, I made my request for a meal, and from there I went to wait where a lady's maid took her meals: the housekeeper's room. I was thankful Mrs. Wilder was not there when I arrived, because breakfast had been an awkward meal.

Several minutes passed, and then the door opened to admit the other housemaid. She had a tray of food in her hands, as though she had expected my request. "Thank you," I said sincerely. The girl made a noncommittal sound as she set it down. "What is your name?"

"Molly," was all she said. There was only indifference in her voice, which seemed a marked improvement on hatred and dislike.

"Molly, perhaps you could tell me something," I said, keeping my gaze on the tray of food. I didn't want her to suspect I was interrogating her. Out of the corner of my eye, I saw Molly pause, and I knew I had her attention. Good. "Why was

Mary overlooked for the position of lady's maid? Miss Burnham clearly prefers her."

In the silence that followed, I lifted my head. Molly was staring, her mouth opened as though my question had shocked her. "Why would you care the reason Mary was ignored?" she demanded once she met my gaze. "You were hired instead of Mary getting promoted. You're better than the rest of us! What does it matter who didn't get promoted?"

"That is for me to be concerned with." I kept my voice even. Not superior or defensive. Just calm. "And I certainly do not think I am better than anyone. Please. Just answer my question."

Maybe it was because I said 'please' or maybe it was because she wanted me to know exactly how angry all of the servants were at the injustice of it. "Because Mrs. Burnham wanted a lady's maid with more sophistication than Mary."

"Sophistication? Oh, I see."

Molly paused and tilted her head. "Do you? Because the rest of us do not," she said sharply. She brushed a lock of her hair back that had fallen into her face. "What makes you more sophisticated than Mary? She's been studying all she can to make advancement."

I couldn't resist a wry smile and shook my head. How to explain the small details a lady's maid needs; the understanding of French, the intricacies of the latest fashions? "Thank you for your honesty, Molly," was all I could think to say.

She eyed me for a moment longer before she left the room, and I was left to eat my toast and drink my tea in peace. The morning had given me a great deal to think about. Eugenia falling for a man who was respectable enough was cause for joy.

Then there was the maid, Mary, being passed over because she lacked the sophistication required for the position.

And I was no closer to clearing my family's name. If Jonathan had been there, he would have accused me of procrastinating.

I shook my head at the direction my thoughts had taken. If Jonathan were alive, I wouldn't even be in this situation. He and my parents would never have let me do anything like this. They would have fought off the rumors another way because they would have been in a position to do so, and I would have been merely a friend to Eugenia, able to lend my support in facing the ton.

How much more comfortable that would have been!

What would my family, or anyone else, say if they saw Juliet Sinclair in this situation?

Mary startled me as she opened the door without looking. "Miss Nelson, Mrs. Burnham has been requesting your assistance. She and Miss Eugenia have returned."

Frowning, I stood up. "They've returned already?"

"As a lady's maid, aren't you supposed to be aware of these things?" she asked, her tone falsely innocent.

An unfair question given that the distance between the dressing room and the housekeeper's room meant I had no way of knowing when Mrs. Burnham walked in. Narrowing my eyes, I met her at the door. "Thank you, Mary." She was shorter than me, her eyes at my chin, and I was fully aware the move forced her to look up at me. "I'm sure you don't want to be kept from your normal duties."

For the briefest of moments, we stared at each other, and I wasn't sure what to expect from her. She finally spun on her heel and stalked away. Shaking my head, I hurried up to the dressing room. Even though I knew how she had been passed over, Mary's behavior made it extremely difficult to feel sorry for her.

"Nelson! Where were you? A carriage struck a puddle and splattered mud all over my dress. I must change quickly so I may visit Lady Jersey and thank her for the invitation," Mrs. Burnham exclaimed as soon as I stepped foot into the dressing room. "Perhaps she will solve the mystery of who petitioned her on our behalf. Come, quickly!"

"I thought you had surmised Mr. Landon was responsible for that."

Mrs. Burnham huffed. "Now that I've had time to consider it, I've decided Eugenia was correct," she said, not giving me any help as I pulled the muddied gown off her. "Though it would have been a romantic gesture, Landon is far too honorable to have done such a thing without a formal engagement being settled upon. So, I must solve the mystery on my own, and Lady Jersey is right where I must begin."

"I am certain you will be successful," I said, less than truthfully. From everything I had heard, Lady Jersey was not one to take questioning very well. The Almack's patroness was fond of jests, and I was reasonably sure she would tell Mrs. Burnham nothing.

"You are a treasure, Julie." My employer sighed as I buttoned up her clean walking dress. "I don't know what I would have done without you."

I couldn't keep from flinching. Her abrupt mood swings were hard to adjust to. And she was back to calling me 'Julie' again. But it was fine. I would become accustomed to it.

ON MY THIRD DAY IN the house, Mrs. Burnham instructed me to go out and purchase ribbons to update a few of her gowns as she wanted to look her best at the upcoming social gatherings. Before I departed, I stood in front of her wardrobe and couldn't help but shake my head at the waste of it all.

If my employer simply ordered me to remove the adornments that already cluttered her gowns, there would be plenty of items I could use to refresh the look of them all with hardly any cost. It would have been the economic decision; however, it was not to be.

Sighing, I took note of the colors that would complement that many shades of pink, as the specifics had been left to my discretion. I knew I would never be able to convince her of my logic, at least not at this point, so what was the point of wasting my breath? At least, I now had a reason to leave the house for a short time.

Even though it was another gray, rainy day, I was a bit excited. It had been less than a week since I had entered the house, but I loathed the feeling of being trapped inside. I was accustomed to being allowed to come and go, in the company of the requisite maid for propriety, as I pleased. Having to stay within four walls? Not exactly the most desirable situation for me to be in, nevermind I had put myself there.

It took only a few moments to slip on my pale gray pelisse and tie my straw bonnet beneath my chin. I secured my reticule to my wrist. Only when I turned to leave did a rush of nerves hit.

I had never gone anywhere alone in London.

I was working up my courage to take my first step when there was a light tap on my door. Breathing out, feeling somewhat relieved at having my departure pushed back even slightly, I pulled it open. "Miss Graham," I said, not surprised to see her standing there. That she was dressed to walk out, though, did give me pause. "How are you today? Are you on your way out?"

"As you appear not to have a concern for propriety at all, I would be remiss in my duties if I did not at least attempt to save you from yourself," she responded, her tone prim and proper to the extreme. Then, she smiled, showing she wasn't truly upset. Or I hoped that's what she meant to convey. "And I have been instructed to direct you to the correct shop for the items you need."

A relieved laugh escaped me. "I will be very glad of your company, Miss Graham," I admitted. "And you caught me just in time. I was about to leave."

With my former governess at my side, I left through the servants' entrance. None of the other servants were in sight, though I heard talking coming from the kitchen area. It seemed as though the hostility had abated, which was a relief. Still, it was clear I was not welcome in the house. The rain had turned to drizzle as we set off down the pavement. Several people, noble and servant, were also taking advantage of the break in the weather.

"How goes your quest, Juliet?"

Glancing over at Miss Graham, I raised my eyebrows. "Quest?" I repeated, highly amused by the term. "You make me sound like one of those knights of old I would read about as a child."

"Quest was the kindest word I could think of. What I was truly thinking...should not be spoken by a lady of any breeding."

I laughed outright. Verbally sparring with Miss Graham had always been a favorite pastime for me, though she would always accuse me of impertinence and scold me for being argumentative. "You are referring, of course, to my idiotic, ill-advised, and headstrong decisions in life?" I asked, my tone teasing. She gave me a sharp look that informed me my levity was not appreciated at this point. "I honestly have not had the opportunity to learn anything. Although..."

Remembering Mr. Harper's odd behavior on my first night in the house caused my voice to trail away. Should I reveal what he had done? I hadn't seen him since then, so did I have cause for concern?

"Although what?" Miss Graham asked a note of impatience in her voice.

I decided honesty was the best course of action. "I was not aware Mr. Oswyn Harper had been staying with the Burnhams. It gave me a start when I saw him. You remember him, don't you? He came to stay with Jonathan one summer, about eight years ago. I crossed paths with him when I was learning my way around the bedrooms."

There was silence from my companion, so I glanced over. Miss Graham had a puzzled, almost outright confused, expression on her face. "Mr. Harper?" she repeated slowly. "Around the bedrooms?"

"Yes," I said, just as slowly as she had spoken. "Is there something wrong?"

"Mr. Harper hasn't stayed with the Burnhams for as long as I've been with them, and there are no guests in the house at all."

My steps faltered, and I reached out to grab her arm. "I saw him go into the Blue Room," I said, keeping my voice low. "And then he went into Mr. Burnham's room. He told me he was retrieving a document of some kind."

Pursing her lips, Miss Graham resumed walking, pulling free of my grasp. Realizing I was the recipient of strange looks, I quickly caught up with her. "You understand my concern? Do I have reason to worry?"

"He could not possibly have a valid reason to be up there," she admitted, frowning thoughtfully. "Mr. Harper assists Mr. Burnham with his papers, and it's true he is often at dinner with the family. He has never needed to stay overnight. And he has not dined with them in the past week."

So, though she wouldn't come out and say it, I did have reason to worry. "What do you think it means?"

She shook her head. "I don't know."

Silence fell between us as we walked. That Miss Graham was concerned made my own disquiet grow. And though there had been many times, as my governess, when she'd admitted to not knowing something, I'd always considered her one of the smartest persons of my acquaintance.

What had Mr. Harper been doing in the house?

"What am I to do now?" Miss Graham wondered aloud. "I feel I must tell someone, but who would believe me? All Mr. Harper would have to do is say he was not there. And yet to do nothing..."

I nodded in understanding. "Perhaps if we were to keep an eye on the situation and see if it happens again," I suggested.

"Or perhaps mention it to Mr. Burnham's valet, Bridge. He was there. In the room, I mean. I saw him go in right before Mr. Harper did."

To my surprise, that bit of information made Miss Graham visibly relax. "Then, there must be a logical explanation for his actions. I understand why you would be suspicious, Juliet, however, Mr. Bridge would never allow an intruder into his domain. As he did not raise a cry at Mr. Harper's entrance, we must assume it was an arranged meeting and all is well."

"An odd meeting place. Even if Bridge did arrange such a meeting, why would he do so in Mr. Burnham's chambers?"

"Honestly, Juliet, you are overly suspicious. I will not have you casting aspersions on a man innocent of any wrongdoing!"

Her outburst took me by surprise, and I stared at her. Her cheeks were flushed, and a tiny suspicion snuck into my mind. "Miss Graham? Do you perchance have a fondness for Mr. Burnham's valet?" I asked in astonishment.

"Don't be ridiculous!" she protested, far too quickly. She made a gesture towards the nearest shop window. "Here. Mrs. Burnham always purchases her ribbons here. She feels the quality is far superior to other establishments."

And with that, she changed the subject altogether. In doing so, she solidified my suspicion into something as good as fact in my mind. After so many years a spinster and governess, Miss Graham was smitten with a man. A valet, of all people.

As I followed her into the shop, I wasn't sure whether to be happy for her or exceedingly disappointed. I was fond of Miss Graham, and I knew she was worthy of a good man's attention. But a valet? She was a thousand times better than a man like that.

If Miss Graham was made happy by the man, though, I would find some way to be happy for her. Of course, I hadn't even given a thought to whether Bridges was even interested in courting her!

Shaking those thoughts from my head, I turned all of my attention towards selecting the ribbons and feathers I had been tasked with acquiring. I was sure I would inevitably make the wrong choice, but I took care in the items I selected. The quality of the merchandise was, indeed, excellent, and it came with an equally dear price.

Out of the corner of my eye, I saw Miss Graham make a few selections herself. And she was not one to dress up her gowns at all. That in itself told me a great deal about her feelings. I made a mental note to learn more about Bridges if I had the opportunity.

What happened next was indeed my fault. I gathered my paper wrapped packages and turned around to remove myself from the clerk who had many customers to tend to. In doing so, I found myself inches from the front of a man's great coat. One currently being worn by a man.

"Pardon me, Miss. It's a bit crowded in here."

That voice. I knew that voice.

Slowly, I lifted my head and recognized the blue eyes that were staring at me in open astonishment. "Juliet—I mean, Miss Sinclair?" he stammered, all confidence vanishing from his voice.

I swallowed hard, my voice shaking as I said, "Mr. Bladen."

Chapter Six

Henry. The man I'd once thought to marry. He hadn't changed at all in the five years since I'd last seen him, at least not at first glance. He was still taller and slimmer than most men. There were lines around his eyes that I didn't remember being there before, but I tried not to allow myself a closer look.

Why was he in a shop like this?

It took me a second to realize that he'd just asked me the same thing and for a moment, my mind was completely blank. "What else does a young woman do in a shop?" I managed to say, holding up the small packages in my hands. I, at least, had a plausible excuse for being there, if it wasn't exactly the most truthful. "I purchased ribbons."

"Who is with you?" Mr. Bladen sent a glance around the small shop. I saw his eyes widen and knew he had seen her. "Can that be Miss Graham?"

"Yes, it is." I was relieved he had answered his own question. "She had purchases of her own to make, and I am waiting for her to complete them."

"She stayed with you, then. I am glad you had some consistency in your life after your parents... Well, I feared she might have been sent off when your uncle came for you."

My fingers tightened around the packages. That was precisely what had happened. How dare he? After leaving and staying away for five years with not a word of explanation, now he tries to tell me he was happy there had been 'consistency' in my life? No. He wasn't going to lie to me, and even if he wasn't lying—I didn't want to hear it. Not from him. Not after so long. "What are you doing here?"

His eyes returned to me, and there was a startled expression on his face. He'd never heard me speak so sharply before. His cheeks flushed red. "Ah, yes. Well, um—" He cleared his throat, and I felt a wicked stab of amusement at his embarrassment. "It's awkward, but I promised Margaret I would pick up some special lace she had ordered."

I didn't believe a word he'd said. How could I have expected an honest answer from him? I should have known better than to have even asked. Margaret was his older and married sister. Why would he play errand boy for her? As kind as he'd been when I knew him—well, when I thought I'd known him—he had never shown any inclination to allow anyone to order him around, especially not for something so trivial such as to pick up ribbons.

"She could not have it delivered? Most women do."

A moment of pure panic showed on his face at my question. "She didn't tell me these things can be delivered! She said it was the height of importance for me to bring them to her today! When I see her again—"

He broke off before he finished his threat. Whether he was telling the truth or not, I didn't— couldn't—feel any sympathy for him. I turned to find Miss Graham. Her back was to me, so she had not yet seen Mr. Bladen standing with me. I couldn't leave without her but was reluctant to cut short her purchases.

"You have been well, then, Miss Sinclair?" Mr. Bladen asked after clearing his throat.

Oh, no. We were not going to begin an awkward conversation of how our respective lives had been for the past five years, and I was in no mood for the politeness required between 'Miss Sinclair' and 'Mr. Bladen' when once we had been so close. "I must return to Miss Graham. She is sure to have finished by now," I said, ignoring the question. "Good day, Mr. Bladen."

He reached out a hand, stopping short of actually touching my arm. "Miss Sinclair, please," he said softly. On the verge of walking away, I paused, hearing a note of pleading in his voice that hadn't been there before. "I-I have missed your company. I hope you know that."

My breath caught in my throat. Why would he say such a thing here? A small part of my heart wanted, desperately, to believe him. He'd left so abruptly that I had expected something terrible had happened in his family. Just like it had with mine. I'd waited in vain for a letter or message. Anything to explain why he'd left when I had needed him the most.

Remembering that time made my chin come up. "I'm afraid I know nothing of the kind, Mr. Bladen," I said, startled at how cold my voice came out. When he took a step back, dropping his hand, I could see he was shocked too. "Good day."

This time, when I turned away, he did not impede me. Miss Graham had finally noticed us. "It's time to return, Miss Graham," I said to her, catching her arm in mine. I practically pulled her from the shop.

"Juliet, was that—" She glanced over her shoulder.

"Yes, it was." I resisted the urge to look back. I was certain he would be there, watching me walk away, and if he wasn't...well, I don't think my heart would be able to stand the pain of that. Again. "He was picking up ribbons for his sister."

"Mrs. Richards?" Miss Graham asked in surprise. "She sent her brother for...ribbons? Why wouldn't they have simply been delivered to her house? Or her maid sent to collect them?"

"That is a question we will never have answered." I kept my gaze firmly forward. I was satisfied with that. Really.

"Juliet, are you well?"

"Yes, of course. We should get back before some other person recognizes who I really am."

Out of the corner of my eye, I noted Miss Graham's face was one of skepticism. She didn't believe me any more than I believed myself. But she didn't say anything, which I was grateful for as I didn't want to talk about it.

RETURNING TO THE BURNHAMS' house, Miss Graham and I went our separate ways: she to discover what mischief her charges had wrought while she was away, and I to the dressing room. I stored the ribbons and lace in the basket at the bottom of the wardrobe. With all the repairs I already had to make, I wasn't too eager to begin refreshing the others.

I selected a gown for the evening and then waited for Mrs. Burnham to return. I certainly had plenty to occupy my mind.

Two faces from my past in less than a week. One, my brother's closest friend from school and the other, the man I once thought I would marry. One knew me, and the other hadn't recognized my face. They both had one thing common: I had met them in places they had no real reason to be. I shook my head as I thought of it.

And, I still had no idea what either of them had been up to. What did it all mean?

Mrs. Burnham demanded all of my attention when she came sweeping into the room not long after I had set everything out. The entire time I curled her hair, she complained about how no one seemed to know who had convinced Lady Jersey to send the tickets, and no one appreciated how much she did for her daughter. Somehow, I managed to make the appropriate sounds of commiseration.

She barely noticed the dress I helped her into and said nothing about the ribbons she'd sent me to acquire. In the end, she breezed out of the room with the simple order for me to see to Eugenia right away.

Breathing out a sigh, I glanced around at the room I would have to straighten up at some point. Leaving it in disarray, even for a short time, did not sit well with me but I fought down the impulse to take the few moments right then. If I had, I would not have been able to give much time to Eugenia.

I slipped into the young lady's room and was not at all surprised to find Mary already there. She heard me first and spun around, inadvertently tugging on Eugenia's hair. The young woman yelped in pain.

"A lady's maid keeps her attention on her work, and avoids causing her mistress discomfort," I said, my tone chiding as I moved forward. Mary scowled at me, her eyes glaring as I came closer. "Turn back around, Mary, if you're going to continue. Otherwise, please release Miss Burnham's hair before you pull it from her head."

I watched her annoyance fade into shock. Then I made a spinning motion with my finger, prompting her to continue with her task. After one more moment, and just when I thought I would have to take over, Mary turned and continued arranging Eugenia's hair into a Grecian style so prevalent in society. Eugenia quietly watched our exchange in the mirror, not saying a word.

I was reasonably sure they had been talking right before I'd come in, but now there was silence in the room. If I dropped a pin, it would sound as loud as a rumble of thunder.

As I observed Mary at work, I noticed her hands were trembling. For all her blustering and annoyance, she was genuinely nervous by my presence there. I came to a quick decision. "Well done, Mary. Perhaps we will make a lady's maid out of you yet. Good evening, Miss Burnham."

Two pairs of eyes stared at me in the mirror as I turned and left the room. Eugenia did not need two of us there, and I had a dressing room to put right.

In all honesty, I was immensely relieved to find Mary wanted the position. There were a few rough spots to be smoothed out, but she would make an excellent replacement when I could finally escape from the household. And, as I didn't expect to be free any time soon, perhaps there would be time to correct Mary's technique and make her ready to advance to the position she desired.

When I opened the dressing room door and found it to be even worse condition than I had left it, I couldn't find the strength to be upset. I heaved a sigh and set to work picking up the scattered gowns. At least I knew Mary wasn't behind it, which narrowed the suspects down by one, and I had to give the culprit credit for being consistent.

I couldn't help but be grateful there was no damage done to the gowns. I even decided a couple of the dresses could do with a trip to the laundry. Once I had the room once again straightened to my standards, I sorted through the soiled garments.

Some I placed in a smaller basket to take with me, and the others I set aside to be handed to the laundress. I should have washed the undergarments instead of going out for the ribbons, but truthfully, it was one of the tasks I knew I would put aside as long as possible. I had a good idea what the soap and water would do to my hands.

"Why didn't you take over?"

My fatigue had caught up with me by then, so Mary's voice startled me. I turned my head to see her in the doorway. There was a genuinely concerned look on her face. "Did you want me to?"

She shook her head. "Of course not. But, why didn't you?"

"Mary, I know how important it is for girls like you to have the chance to advance." I was unable to keep the tiredness from my voice. "I think you'll make an excellent lady's maid for Miss Burnham when she marries and sets up a household of her own. I'm to look after her needs second to her mother. You can put her first right now, and she won't forget that."

Mary frowned. "Why should you care whether I am promoted or not?"

I hesitated, not knowing what to say. "You wouldn't believe me if I told you," I said with a sigh. Her frown became deeper, and she opened her mouth to say more. I held my hand up to stop her. "Believe me when I say this, though, all I wish to see is Miss Burnham established happily."

To my surprise, Mary stepped into the room and knelt down next to me. "I'll have these for you in the morning, Miss Nelson," she said, taking the basket of undergarments from my hands.

"Why would you do that?"

Her cheeks flushed red. "Because of all the lady's maids who have come through here, I think you want to help Miss Eugenia," she said, looking and sounding uncomfortable. "They would never let me look after her, and she was neglected."

"You're very fond of Miss Burnham, aren't you?"

She lifted her shoulder in a shrug. "We're the same age, and I came here when I was seven to be trained as a maid. We practically grew up together in this house."

I nodded, understanding the bond between them. It sometimes happened, though in my home, all of the maids had been much older than me and the housekeeper kept them strictly respectful at all times. "Then, maybe you can tell me something. How attached is Miss Eugenia to this Gerard Landon?"

Instantly, Mary's face lost all openness, and she shook her head. "Good night, Miss Nelson," she said stiffly. She stood up and left the room.

I was right back where I had started, but Mary's reaction was answer enough. My instinct was right. Eugenia was more than slightly interested in the man. Sighing, I picked myself off the floor. If Eugenia wanted Landon as her future husband, I would need to come up with a strategy for how to help her accomplish that.

For the first time, I began to feel I had taken too much on myself. I wanted to protect my family name. I wanted to help Eugenia. I wanted to find some sense of purpose and happiness in my life.

But how to accomplish all of that?

With nothing left to do, and no desire to return to my needlework just yet, I took myself off to the library. The room was smaller than I remembered, and though it was well-maintained, I had the feeling it was seldom used. I scanned the titles contained on the shelf and found nothing of interest. I returned to my room, and the volume I had brought with me.

This was one of the downsides for a lady's maid. I could not sleep until I had put my mistress to bed for the night. It took all of my willpower to remain awake until the family returned some time past midnight.

Mrs. Burnham was tired and in an unpleasant mood when I helped her undress. She had nothing but complaints about how the dinner party had been, and everything I did resulted in angry outbursts. It was with relief I left her and went to Eugenia's room. Mary was, surprisingly, nowhere in sight, and Eugenia sat at her dressing table.

There seemed to be a bleak look in her eyes when I took the brush from her hand. "Is there something wrong, Miss Burnham?" I asked as I began brushing her hair. I grimaced as the bristles became tangled. Her hair was in sore need of some change. Something to make it more manageable.

"My mother expects so much of me," Eugenia said, seeming not to notice I was tugging on her hair in what had to be a painful manner. "And she keeps telling everyone I will make a brilliant match. And all of them give me such calculating looks!

The kind that says I am not pretty enough to even think I will make a good marriage!"

"What do appearances have to do with it?" I asked calmly. How well I remembered feeling much the same when I was faced with the critical looks from the ton. "Do you believe that to be the only way to win a husband?"

"I know I will never be a diamond of the first water, like Mama hopes," Eugenia said, ignoring my questions. "I'm not charming, or witty, or even flirtatious!"

Setting aside the brush, I began to separate her hair into three equal sections. "Then, you will be certain the man who does offer for you does so for you, and not for your beauty or wealth." I started braiding her thick and heavy hair. There had to be something I could do to make it easier to work with!

"Why must I even go to the parties, and dinners and balls?" Eugenia asked, her tone petulant. "All the other girls do is flirt with any eligible man who comes near, and I can only speak to the people I have been introduced to. I would much rather spend my time with Miss Graham and Mary."

Her maid and her governess? Those were the only two she considered her friends? Oh, dear. "You must never let your mother hear you say such a thing, you know. It would give her an attack of the nerves, I am sure."

She laughed, her eyes losing the bleakness I'd seen in the mirror. "Yes, I suppose it would," she said. She heaved a sigh. "Oh, why must growing up be so difficult? I shudder to think of how I longed to be old enough for a London season when I was young!"

Leaning forward, I picked up a ribbon to tie off the braid. "I'm afraid growing up is an unforgivable fact of life." I rested a comforting hand on her shoulder for a brief moment. "Will there be anything else, Miss Burnham?"

"No. Good night, Miss Nelson."

My evening finally over, I left her chamber. The house was far quieter than I had ever heard before as I made my way to my room. Thankfully, no further mischief had been done there, and I was able to ready myself for bed. I was asleep within moments of laying my head down.

Chapter Seven

And it all began again the next morning. Somehow, even though I'd settled into the routine, it became much harder to rise each morning when Mary knocked on my door. Once I had order restored, there was little I needed to do in the dressing room, which was fortunate because it took longer each day for my mind to become clearer. My steps were slow as I went down to collect the first tray I had to deliver to Eugenia.

On the first day I had to myself, the cook said nothing when I nearly tripped over a chair leg. She did, however, give me a sympathetic look. When I returned upstairs, it took me several minutes to rouse Eugenia. I suspected she must have lain awake during the night, and she mumbled incomprehensibly when I shook her shoulder. I understood completely, but if I had to face the day, so did she.

In the end, the mention of chocolate finally convinced her to sit up, and I could leave the room, confident she wouldn't fall back to sleep. Then I descended to the kitchen, with a quick detour for the morning's correspondence. I picked up the tray for Mrs. Burnham and started up the stairs again.

I should have known disaster would strike; I felt only half awake, and what better time for misfortune to come around? My foot caught the edge of the step, and I tumbled forward. The fine china toppled off the tray, which I'd let go of in an attempt to catch myself, and shattered on the steps. My right hand curled around the railing, saving myself from hitting the hard stone steps.

A cry of pain erupted from my lips as my shoulder jarred upon landing. The sound of tearing fabric accompanied my cry. Well, at least it had woken me completely. I pulled myself upright and groaned as I took in the mess now covering the stairs. Quickly, I snatched up the correspondence that was in danger of being ruined and waved the letters in the air to remove the liquid from the paper. There was the squeak of a door opening below as I knelt to clear the rest of the mess.

"Are you well, Miss Nelson?"

My hands stilled at the voice. Mr. Harper. Why was he here at this time of day? Slowly, I twisted around to look at the young man standing at the bottom of the stairs. He had his coat on, as though he'd been on the verge of going out, or Wilder had neglected to take it from him when he'd come in; something that didn't seem likely.

"I-I'm not hurt," I managed to stammer out when I realized he was staring at me. "It was simply an accident."

"Let me help you." He put his foot on the first step.

Two of us in this small space? Not a chance! "No, no. I can manage, sir," I said swiftly, struggling to keep the panic out of my voice. The more he and I interacted, the more likely it was he would recognize me. I was relieved to see Mary come into view behind him, no doubt drawn by the noise of my fall. "Oh, Mary. I missed the step and dropped Mrs. Burnham's tray."

Mr. Harper turned and stepped aside to allow the maid to reach me. She gave me a puzzled look as she climbed the stairs. "You go on up to the mistress, Miss Nelson," Mary said, nudging me with her shoulder. Maybe she could tell I didn't want to be there. In any event, I was extremely grateful for her rescue. "I will have the cook prepare another tray and bring it up to you."

"Thank you," I said, straightening up. I nodded once in Mr. Harper's direction. "Good day, sir."

There was a frown on his face when I turned to hurry on my way. The clink of china fragments landing on the tray echoed behind me. I breathed out as I stepped into the hallway. Yet another unexpected encounter with someone from my past. Lovely. Just lovely.

No one made visits this early in the day. No doubt an argument could be made he had a reason for doing so, something to do with assisting Mr. Burnham. But to twice find him where he should not have been...I couldn't help but feel suspicious.

I had come to the Burnham house to solve my own problems, but it seemed I had stumbled onto a plot in need of resolving. And I had done little to achieve my own objective. I'd hardly had time to even think! There were too many mysteries in this house to distract me from my original plan to clear my family's name.

Reaching Mrs. Burnham's door, I paused, taking a calming breath. I couldn't forget why I was doing all of this in the first place, but I also needed to focus on my duties. Somehow, I had to find a way to make it all balance out.

WITH SUCH A START TO the day, I was more than ready for my afternoon off. I had Mrs. Burnham dressed to receive any visitors. Eugenia had left for an afternoon walk with Miss Graham, and my time was once again my own.

I couldn't keep from humming as I changed into the nicest gown I had allowed myself to bring. It was a pale green, and simple enough to pass as a lady's maid's gown, excellent though it was. I tied on my bonnet and slipped into my pelisse. All that remained was for me to get outside and commence my walk without being seen.

It would be simple enough to explain my attire. I could claim it was a gift from a former employer, though there would bound to be questions about where I could be going alone dressed in such finery. My steps were quick as I made my way out. Thankfully, it was clear all the way to the door.

The day was beautiful, which was a relief as visiting in bad weather would not have been enjoyable. The sun was shining, though weakly and many clouds were drifting through the sky. I took a deep breath as I set out on my way, happy to be able to enjoy it at my leisure.

It was less than an hour's walk from Harley Street to Great George Street, necessary to avoid St. James Street where there would be more people walking. I kept my steps quick and steady, not wanting anyone to notice a woman alone. I recognized the street as soon as I stepped foot on it. It was even quieter than the one the Burnham's house was on, and there was hardly anyone in sight.

I took a moment on the sidewalk to look up at the house. It looked exactly as I had left it. The windows were covered with curtains, so Aunt Beth must have been having a bad day as she did now and again. I stepped through the gate, flinching as the iron protested loudly at the motion.

Aunt Beth had spent the last two decades in this house with only a modest income to survive on, and it had already begun to show. I felt a surge of anger at my uncle, who hadn't cared to maintain the house as he should have. He was the head of the family. And where was he? In Egypt, searching for relics of a time long past.

When I rapped the knocker, I knew I would have to wait several minutes. The staff my aunt kept were getting on in years, and there were never any visitors. Carlson finally opened the door, and his eyebrows rose when he saw me.

"Miss Juliet," he said, stepping back to allow me in. "You have returned. Miss Beth will be pleased."

"I'm only here for a few hours, Carlson." I removed my pelisse and bonnet to hand them over to his care. I turned in a circle in the hall, breathing in the scent of Faircroft. There was the slightest hint of musk and a closed-off smell I'd forgotten about. "How is my aunt?"

"She has had a headache for the past week, Miss Juliet," he said in his grave tone of voice. There was an unspoken implication of 'ever since you left' in his tone. "Shall I announce you?"

I shook my head. "No, I'll surprise her. Is she in the drawing room?"

"Yes, Miss Juliet."

With all the windows covered, it was dim in the house as I made my way to the door of the drawing room. Hopefully, I would be able to tease her out of her doldrums.

"Aunt Beth," I said as I opened the door. "It's Juliet."

The drawing room was darker than I'd ever seen it. Aunt Beth's mood was worse than I'd thought. After a moment, there was a response. "Juliet? You've come home?" Aunt Beth's voice was weak and fragile. "Oh, I thought this day would never come."

Squinting, I thought I saw her lounging on the chaise nearest to the fireplace. "I told you I would come to visit, Auntie," I said, feeling my way across the room. I crossed to the farthest window and pulled the curtains open. "It's only been a few days."

"So, you haven't come to your senses?"

Disappointment was evident in her voice, and I bit back a sigh as I moved to the next window. "I'm beginning to feel I ought to be in Bedlam Asylum the way everyone keeps questioning my sanity," I said lightly as I opened the third set of drapes. Finally, the room was bright, and I smiled at the feel of the sun shining in.

"You mustn't jest about Bedlam! If Frederick ever finds out about this mad scheme of yours, that is exactly where he will send you!"

Turning around, I forced out a bitter laugh. "Uncle Frederick has been in Egypt for nearly five years, Aunt Beth. Even if he were to make a sudden return home, I hardly think he will discover what I've been doing, much less care."

Aunt Beth had sat up, regarding me with concern. "Juliet, Frederick is family. Of course he cares what you do, especially when it involves you endangering your reputation!"

Raising my eyebrow, I took a seat opposite my aunt. We'd discussed this—well, argued would be a more appropriate word—many times in the past five years. "He has a strange way of showing familial concern." I held my hand up when it looked as though she would continue the conversation. "I'm only here for a short time, Aunt. Can we not talk about this?"

"I wish you would give up on this foolish plot, you errant minnow," Aunt Beth said, twisting a handkerchief in her hands.

"Have you learned anything that will bring this farce to an end?"

Pursing my lips, I hesitated. "Not yet, but I do feel as though I am doing something useful with my life, Aunt. It feels good."

"If you wanted to feel useful, you could have sewn clothing for charity, like any other well-bred young woman." Aunt Beth squinted at the window as if noticing I'd opened all the curtains. "When did the sun come out? I must take advantage of it and take a walk."

I grimaced at the thought of another walk so soon. "Shall we see what has bloomed in the garden? We could sit on one of the benches and take in the sun."

"No, let's sit here," Aunt Beth said, apparently changing her mind. "Will you tell me what you've been up to this past week? All I received from you was one letter and a day later than you promised. I could hardly sleep that night, I'll have you know."

She placed her hand at the base of her throat as though she was overcome with emotion. The move had a dramatic flair that made me laugh. "You have never had a restless night's sleep in your life," I said, unable to keep the grin from my face. "It's been interesting at the Burnhams'. There were some things I wasn't expecting, but I'm doing well enough at the job, I believe."

"Don't think I'm going to be proud of you for that."

"Crossing paths with Mr. Harper and Mr. Bladen did give me pause," I continued, ignoring her comment. She didn't mean it, and I wanted to get the hard part over with. "And I found them both in places one would not expect to find young gentlemen."

Aunt Beth gaped at me. "Henry Bladen? Isn't that the loggerheaded miscreant—?"

"Yes," I said, interrupting before she could continue the insult. "He is."

"Oh, my," was all she said for a moment. Her eyes widened. "He didn't recognize you, did he?"

Smiling at her concern, I nodded. "He did. I was at a shop on an errand for Mrs. Burnham, and he came in to fetch an order of ribbons for his sister. Miss Graham, my old governess, was with me, so he had no reason to think I was anyone but myself. You may rest easy on that account, Aunt."

"Well, I must say that is an odd place to meet a man," Aunt Beth said, frowning. "Who sends their brother to play errand boy? I would say a sweet, good man would do so for his sister, but such a man does not exist!"

A laugh escaped me once again. "It was strange, and the last thing I expected to happen."

"Did you speak to him?"

"Well, I ran into him, so it would have been difficult to avoid exchanging words."

Aunt Beth's eyes narrowed. "Juliet, I am aware this is the man who broke your heart, but I do hope you at least had the sense not to be rude."

"Rude? Me? Must you doubt me so much?" I heaved a sigh as I looked away. "No, I was polite, if you can believe it. He expressed his happiness I had some consistency in my life. He thinks Miss Graham stayed with me after..." My throat seemed to choke me, and I cleared it. "And then he said the oddest thing. That he had missed my company."

My aunt's hand flew to her mouth as she gasped. "He said that?"

"It means nothing, Aunt. I imagine he was being polite."

"Politeness would be saying he is pleased to see you well or some such pleasantry. This is something else entirely. It must mean something, or he wouldn't have said it."

I waved my hand. "Aunt, you know as well as I those in society often say things they do not mean. You cannot read too much into it. I refuse to believe he meant it at all. Not after five years of silence."

The drawing room door swung open and Carlson entered, a tray in his shaking hands. I was never more thankful for a distraction. "Tea, madame," he said in his dignified way. I winced as the china rattled most alarmingly. "Shall I bring anything else?"

"No, thank you, Carlson. Juliet will pour."

Nodding, Carlson turned and made his way out. He, like the other faithful servants in Aunt Beth's household, was not getting any younger. I could only wonder how long they would be able to remain at their posts. What would become of them, and who would we get to take their places?

Shaking off the gloomy thoughts, I stood and moved over to take my place behind the tray. "That other name you mentioned, Harper, was it? I don't think I've heard it before," Aunt Beth said. "No sugar for me, dear. Who is he?"

"He was a friend and schoolmate of Jonathan's." I handed a cup over to her. "He stayed with us several times when Jonathan came home from school in the summer. The last time I saw him was about eight years ago if I am not mistaken."

Aunt Beth looked thoughtful as she sipped her tea. "Does he come from a good family?"

I was not at all surprised by the question. "Aunt Beth! You're not trying to play matchmaker, are you? It's been at least eight years since I last saw him...as Juliet Sinclair, I mean. He knows me as Julie Nelson, a lady's maid. A marriage between us simply wouldn't work."

Scowling, Aunt Beth shook her head. "I knew your thoughtless actions would have horrible consequences. What will you do when you return to society?"

"Do you honestly think someone who has seen me a mere two times in the last eight years will recognize me?" I asked in astonishment. "Aunt, I hardly think I am as memorable as all that."

She sighed. "Please don't tell me you met this one in a shop. Or a market!"

"A lady's maid doesn't need to go to the market, Auntie," I said with a fond smile. "And no. I met him at the Burnhams.'" I frowned as I recalled the circumstances. "Although it was at odd times when he wasn't supposed to be there, and in places he had no logical reason to be in."

"What do you mean?"

I opened my mouth to explain, but the drawing room doors swung open, interrupting our conversation. "A Mr. Bladen to see you, Miss Rycroft," Carlson said. "Shall I show him in?"

Chapter Eight

Startled, I gasped, and Aunt Beth choked on her tea. She began coughing, and I reached for her in concern. She waved my hand away. "Yes, thank you, Carlson," she managed to say once she recovered herself a moment later. "Please show him in and have fresh tea brought up for us."

Giving a slight bow, Carlson stepped back and made a gesture. Mr. Bladen was right behind him? Alarmed, I surged to my feet, setting my teacup aside. Aunt Beth rose more gracefully, not even a hint of the pitiful sight she'd presented when I first arrived.

And then Henry Bladen walked through the doorway. He offered a formal bow, his eyes on me. "Miss Sinclair. Forgive me for intruding."

"Aunt Beth, please allow me to introduce Mr. Bladen," I said, remembering my manners with a jolt. Though I had spoken of Mr. Bladen many times to her, mostly to bewail his abandonment of me when I needed him, he had never been introduced to my aunt. A fact which made his sudden visit strange indeed. "Mr. Bladen, this is my aunt, Miss Rycroft."

"Miss Rycroft."

"I'm pleased to finally get to meet you in person at long last, Mr. Bladen," Aunt Beth said, her tone all graciousness and politeness. "Please, won't you sit down."

He sent a quick glance at me as he took a seat in the chair next to Aunt Beth's couch. I sank back into my seat, making sure I was as far away from him as possible without being blatantly rude. Clearing her throat, Aunt Beth made sure she had our guest's attention.

"What brings you here, Mr. Bladen?" she asked, her tone sweet yet curious. "I don't believe you and I were ever introduced before today, and yet, here you are on a social visit."

There was one thing I loved about Aunt Beth. Her age allowed her to say what she wanted and ask the important questions without being looked down upon. "I realized I hadn't paid my respects to you," Henry—Mr. Bladen—said. "My family would never forgive me if they knew."

I barely kept from an unladylike snort. After five years of silence, this was the excuse for his visit? That his family would be mortified if they discovered he hadn't done so this Season? What made this year so different from the previous ones? Why now must he pay his respects?

"Unbelievable."

"Did you say something, Juliet?" Aunt Beth asked pointedly.

Looking up, I said as sweetly as possible given the circumstances, "I said you must give our greetings to your family, Mr. Bladen. I have had no news of them in —oh, it must be five years now."

Aunt Beth's lips quirked and she raised an eyebrow at my not so subtle criticism. "Yes, of course," Mr. Bladen said, sounding flustered. He glanced at me again. "My mother has spoken of you often though, I do assure you."

His mother. I had grown fond of her in the few times we had met. She was a sweet, caring lady if a bit frail from age and illness. I had looked forward to being a daughter to her and spending many hours at her side.

But that happy event had never happened.

Still, I couldn't allow my disappointed hopes to destroy a friendship I held dear. "I often think of her, and I wish you would tell her so for me."

Mr. Bladen looked straight at me. "I will." The sincerity in his voice sounded so like the young man I had dreamed of spending the rest of my life with my heart ached.

That realization unsettled me more than I thought it could have. I didn't want to remember those dreams and hopes because with those memories came the reminder of what had happened next. He had left, and five years had passed before I ever saw him again. And now, here he was, sitting in Aunt Beth's drawing room and speaking to me.

I had completely missed what he'd just said. "I'm sorry, I wasn't attending," I said swiftly as Aunt Beth glared. "What did you say?"

"I merely remarked I expected to see your uncle, Mr. Rycroft, when I arrived," Mr. Bladen said. "He seemed to be a gentleman most concerned about the company you keep."

An edge had come into his voice I didn't understand. "I wasn't aware you were acquainted with my uncle, Mr. Bladen."

"We had occasion to meet five years ago. He is not in residence?"

I couldn't keep from frowning at his sudden change in attitude.

"My nephew has been in Egypt for several years," Aunt Beth said. "I'll be sure to mention you in my next letter to him, and extend your regards to Frederick."

Mr. Bladen inclined his head in acceptance, but I noticed the way his jaw clenched. Had he and my uncle had a disagreement? Uncle Frederick had never mentioned he'd spoken to Mr. Bladen. Was my uncle the reason behind Mr. Bladen's departure?

Puzzled, I had nothing else to say for the rest of his brief visit. He declined any refreshment Aunt Beth offered and left after ten minutes of awkward, stilted conversation with my aunt.

"Well, what an interesting young man," she said, looking immensely pleased for some reason. "I can see why you lost your heart to him, Juliet. He is a handsome one."

"Handsome is as handsome does, Aunt." I pushed myself out of my chair and went to the window, watching him walk through the gate. Not wishing to be caught spying, I hovered behind the curtain. He might think—why did I care what he thought? Feeling confused, I moved back to my chair. "Let us not forget he is the one who left me without a word of explanation."

"Perhaps you will have that explanation now," Aunt Beth said, her tone stubborn. "You cannot judge him when you know nothing of the circumstances!"

"And I cannot trust him for the same reason." Lifting up my teacup, which I had barely touched during Mr. Bladen's entire visit, I sipped the liquid without really thinking about it.

"Now, why do you have that look on your face?" Aunt Beth narrowed her eyes at me.

"Do you think—could Uncle Frederick be the reason Mr. Bladen left?" I asked, getting straight to the heart of my concern. "Uncle Frederick never mentioned meeting Mr. Bladen, but he must have known o-of my hopes and expectations."

Aunt Beth poured herself more tea. "Why would Frederick scare away a prospective match? No, I cannot believe he would do such a thing, not when it is his responsibility to see you happily settled."

Scoffing, I shook my head. "Well, he hasn't exactly made any effort to accomplish that objective now, has he?"

"He is also occupied with his work," Aunt Beth exclaimed in protest. "He has always been busy with his studies. Once he returns from the dig, I'm sure he will do everything in his power to find you a husband, or put you in the way of finding a husband."

Raising my eyebrow, I forced a laugh. "Somehow, I don't think I want the kind of husband Uncle Frederick will choose for me. Some priggish professor of something or other? No, thank you."

"You cannot know Frederick would choose one of his colleagues."

Sometimes, there was just no way to reason with her. I sipped my tea again, wrinkling my nose as I realized it was cold. Setting it down I sent a glance towards the clock on the mantel. "I must get back before I am missed," I said with a mixture of regret and relief.

"You only just arrived! We haven't had a chance to talk, Juliet!"

"I'm sorry, but this is how it has to be." I went to her side and placed a kiss on her cheek. "I will return on my next free day. And I promise I will write if anything happens."

Aunt Beth scowled at me. "There is a letter for you." She selected it from the table beside her. "I do hope you will be able to spare a moment to read it in your busy days to come."

Nothing I could have said right then would appease her. I accepted the message from her hand and tucked it into my reticule as I turned to leave.

"Simmons will take you. Tell him where to pick you up next time as well. I can't have you walking so far alone. Who knows what would happen to you?"

"You know I cannot allow that, Aunt," I said, pausing in the doorway. Even when she was irritated with me, she couldn't help but show her concern for my welfare. "It would draw too much attention to me. Now, try not to exert yourself too much while I am away."

Carter stood in the hall with my pelisse and bonnet in her hands. "Miss Juliet," she said, keeping her expression neutral. She couldn't hide the curiosity in her eyes, though.

"Hello, Carter," I said with a smile. As I tied my bonnet on, it occurred to me she was the perfect person to help me with my knotty problem. "If you were in charge of dressing a head of unfortunate thick, curly hair, how would you manage it?"

The maid's eyebrow raised. "Are you finding your work troublesome, Miss Juliet?"

"More than I thought I would." I kept my tone low. "I know how to fix the unflattering state of her wardrobe, but her hair is impossible!"

"Has the young lady considered cutting it?"

CARTER'S SUGGESTION remained with me as I returned to the Burnham household. Miss Burnham and her mother were out, and I found myself with time on my hands. Returning to my room, I set myself to make further repairs to Mrs. Burnham's wardrobe.

As I occupied myself with my thread and needle, there was a knock on my door. "Yes, who is it?" I asked, looking up from the delicate repair I was attempting on the hem of one of the dresses. I waited a few moments before I tried again. "Yes? Hello?"

No answer. Shaking my head, I turned my attention back to my work. A second later, there was another knock, louder than before. "Yes?" I said, lifting my head once more. No response and I clenched my jaw. "If this is someone's idea of a prank, I warn you I am not amused!"

Still, nothing was said from the hallway. Standing up, I set aside my work and moved carefully to the door without making a sound. When there came, as I had suspected there would, a third knock, I grabbed the doorknob and swung the door wide.

Startled, Daphne and Calliope fell onto their backsides in the hallway. "Is there something you wish, Miss Daphne, Miss Calliope?" I speared them with my best interpretation of Miss Graham's most disapproving glare.

"Well, we just wanted to know what you're doing," Daphne said, scrambling up first. She stepped forward as if she were going to come into my room.

I blocked her way. "I am working. What are you doing?"

They exchanged glances. "We want to see," Calliope said, joining her sister. Her hair was an abominable mess. "Step aside and let us in, Nelson."

"I will not." I pulled the door closed so that only half of me was in the doorway. "Shouldn't you be with Miss Graham?"

"Ol' Gray Boots is on a walk with Genie," Daphne said, trying to push on the door. Quite honestly, her behavior was closer to that expected from a three-year-old, not a fifteen-year-old, and her nickname for Miss Graham was hardly flattering. "This is our house, and you have to do what we tell you!"

I had never dealt well with children. At least, not ones who were old enough to walk and talk and generally make nuisances of themselves. I much preferred adorable babies who slept most of the time, though even then I'd had little contact with the creatures.

So being faced with two teenage girls who behaved like spoiled toddlers, was quickly grating on my nerves.

"Unfortunately for you, that's not quite true." My words caused confused looks to cross their faces. Clearly, they were not accustomed to not having their own way. "You see, I was given this room to stay in while I'm here, therefore it belongs to me and I can choose who to allow in."

"It doesn't work like that!" Calliope said in protest.

"It does, in fact, work like that. If you don't like it, I suggest you find your father and ask him."

The girls exchanged looks. They seemed to hold a silent conversation and then turned away. They raced down the corridor, and I pulled myself back into my room, leaning against the door with a sigh of relief.

I had no doubt they would return. Hazarding a guess, I surmised they were desperate for attention and didn't care what kind or where it came from. Mrs. Burnham seemed caught up in marrying Eugenia to the wealthiest man she could while avoiding unnecessary inconvenience. Their father being away so much did not help the situation; not that he'd have any interest in them were he there.

Deep down, I did feel sorry for the girls. But they were not the reason I was there. If I could, I would do something for them but I had no intention of being in the house long enough for them to grow up.

Of course, my second objective was to help Eugenia, and I still had yet to find a way to gain her trust. I knew Miss Graham would never betray the girl's confidence, so I could not expect anything from her on the matter.

My thoughts were interrupted by another knock on the door. "Yes?" There was no answer. Spinning around, I pulled the door open. No one stood right in front of the door, so I poked my head out. To my left was Daphne and to my right was Calliope.

"Is there something I can do for you, Miss Daphne, Miss Calliope?" I asked in an all too formal tone of voice.

"You can let us in," Daphne said as if the matter was obvious.

Without a doubt, I knew they weren't going to leave me alone. I sighed, considering just how much work I would be able to do if I tried to ignore them. It wouldn't be that much. "Perhaps if you asked nicely, I might do so."

Again, they looked at each other, this time with surprise. "Ask...nicely?" Calliope repeated as though the words were foreign.

"Yes."

Daphne frowned. "Let us in. Please?" she said, slowly.

I shook my head, unable to keep a smile off my face. "That's not asking nicely. That was telling in a nice-ish way. You both have to ask politely."

Miss Graham was a stickler for manners, so they must be familiar with the concept. But I had the feeling their governess was the only one who ever enforced it.

"May we please come in?" Daphne asked, dragging out each word.

Shifting my gaze to the older girl, I waited. Calliope scowled. "Will you please let us in, Miss Nelson?"

I took a full minute to consider their request, and they both fidgeted more and more. "Very well," I finally said, stepping back. "You may sit with me and practice your stitches. That ought to keep you both out of trouble."

"I hate sewing," Calliope declared, pushing her way in ahead of her sister. "There's always going to be someone else to do it for me, so why should I bother?"

I could sympathize completely, but I wasn't going to let her know that.

She jumped onto my bed, trying to bounce. Daphne went straight to my trunk and opened it. "Did I give you permission to touch my things?" I said as I moved back to my chair. I'd planned on working with some intricate sewing but guessed a more basic task would suit them better. "I will have to ask you to leave if you do not behave yourselves."

Calliope flopped back on my bed, but Daphne obediently closed my trunk and came over. "What are you doing?"

"I am getting the socks for you to darn."

"I won't do your darning!" she said, a whining note in her voice. "It's so boring! You will have to do something else with us."

My eyes must have been sparking with annoyance when I looked at her because she flinched away. "Miss Daphne, this is what you were so desperate to watch. I told you when you came in you would be sewing. Did you think I was jesting?"

Her nose wrinkled with disgust, but she sat down on the floor and took the sock into her hands. "I want Ol' Gray Boots to come back," she said as she stabbed the needle into the sock. "She always pays more attention to Genie than she does us."

"Perhaps if you were kinder to her, she might be willing to give you more attention," I said, falling back on my list of what grown-ups were supposed to say. "Then again, you'll have her full attention once your sister is married."

"Who would want to marry Eugenia?" Calliope asked from where she still lounged on my bed.

I hesitated to include her in the conversation, feeling a strong desire to punish her for ignoring my warning not to touch my things. "Your sister is a pretty girl," I said, keeping my eyes on my work. "All young ladies aim to make excellent matches."

"So, why didn't you?"

My jaw clenched. *Henry.* Would I never be able to think of the man without making my heart hurt? I was still angry with him, as today had proved.

"Silly, servants don't get married!" Daphne objected before I could say a thing. "Besides, she just said young ladies want to find a match, and she's not a lady."

That made me laugh, even though I was aware she was insulting me, and the old pain faded away once again. "If that's the case, then how do you explain Mr. and Mrs. Wilder? You don't imagine they were always married, do you?"

Daphne's hands went still as she frowned. "I don't want to think about it!"

"Then, why aren't you married?" Calliope asked, sliding off the bed.

"There was someone, once," I said, hoping the admission would be enough to keep her satisfied. "But it didn't work out between us and so, here I am."

To my surprise, Daphne reached out and patted my hand. "Maybe you'll find someone else, like father's valet! You're not old, Nelson. And some men like older women, do they not?"

If I had been drinking anything, I would have choked on it. "How do you know about that?"

She lifted a shoulder in a shrug. "Mama says if father ever dies, she'll find someone who appreciates the charms of an older, experienced woman," she said, her tone matter of fact. Daphne pulled her hand back and continued with the rather poor repair of the sock in her hand. "But I hope nothing ever happens to father."

For the second time in five minutes, I felt a twinge in my chest. "That's good," I managed to say. "You need to appreciate your parents. You never know when they might be taken away from you."

"I'm so bored," Calliope wailed, ignoring my heartfelt advice completely.

"I have more needles, and there are plenty of things in need of repair."

She groaned, stretching her hand out. "Fine, but you can't tell Ol' Gray Boots! If you do, I'll-I'll put bugs in your bed!"

I raised an eyebrow. "First of all, of course, I will not tell her. The only reason I would have to reveal your presence here to Miss Graham is if you cause trouble. Other than that, whatever happens in this room, stays in this room. Second, why should Miss Graham not know of your activity if you do it well? Thirdly, you should never warn someone what you plan to do to them. You'll just give them time to retaliate."

Her eyes widened. "Retaliate?"

"How do you know so much about it?" Daphne asked in awe.

"Because I'm smart, that's why," was my rather inelegant response to that. "Now, start sewing."

Chapter Nine

Once they settled down to their task, the girls became rather calm. They chatted easily about a few of the things Miss Graham had been teaching them. I realized with some surprise that they were fond of their governess, a situation I would not have guessed at given how they detested her presence. I learned Daphne had a love for history, while Calliope preferred to read. Both were emphatic in their dislike of French, Italian, and the pianoforte.

I sent them on their way when it neared the hour to dress Mrs. Burnham for her evening. She and Eugenia were to join another family at the opera. No doubt the idea was to display Eugenia in the box for all to see.

I was aware that few went to the opera house to savor the music. I, admittedly, had been more interested in the sights to be seen when I had attended, even though I enjoyed a musical performance as much as the next person. Going to the shops for fabric and ribbons, walking in St. James' Park, and exploring the wonders contained in the British Museum had been my favorite activities to spend my time.

Bracing myself for my task, I made my way up to the dressing room. I flinched at the gown that Mrs. Burnham had already selected. It was, for once, not pink, but a garish gold that

I knew instantly would look horrible on her. The multitude of bows, of the same color, did not help to flatter her appearance.

If this was where Eugenia received her sense of fashion, the poor girl truly needed help. Especially if she never had a reliable lady's maid to guide her. I knew without being told that Mrs. Burnham would never accept the opinion of the dressmaker, who would know what would and would not compliment a woman's figure.

Perhaps that was the first place I could start with Eugenia. She would feel more confident if she knew she looked her best and the first step in that direction would be dresses that suited her. On that note, I would have to do something different with her hair, perhaps trying for an entirely different style; one that was also popular. It wasn't that long hair was out of fashion, but Eugenia's hair would not hold a curl for longer than a few minutes and those curls were necessary for the usual hairstyles.

Mrs. Burnham would have a conniption fit when she learned my plans. Hopefully, I would be able to swear Eugenia to secrecy long enough for me to be able to make it happen. And then, there would be little Mrs. Burnham could do about it.

With that thought in mind, I worked through Mrs. Burnham's complaints and demands. I had a suspicion that the attitude of the servants wasn't all that prevented the house from keeping a lady's maid in residence.

Since that last night I had seen Mary working with Eugenia's hair, the maid hadn't been in sight near the young lady's bedroom. Thankfully Eugenia had changed into one of the few gowns that suited her: a pale blue that matched her eyes. "Nelson, you're here," she said in relief. Her hair was loose as though she'd attempted to arrange it herself.

"Your mother had specific needs." What else could I say? Nothing that wouldn't be taken as rudeness or complaining. "Allow me to take over, Miss Burnham."

"Mama was demanding." Eugenia relinquished the hairbrush to me with a sigh. "I know her all too well."

"Yes, I suppose you would." I couldn't waste time with anything fancy, and I wasn't entirely sure if her hair would cooperate if I even attempted. "I'm going to be completely honest with you; we can't keep doing this."

Eugenia's face screwed up with a mixture of emotions. "I knew I was a hopeless case."

"That's not what I said." I hadn't meant for her to take my words that way at all. "I meant that we're going to have to try something different with your hair."

"But what else can we do?"

"We can discuss it sometime when you do not have to go to the opera." Carter had given me a tiny hope, but I wasn't sure if it would work or not. I would need to send a message before I could hint at there being a plan. I threaded a ribbon through her hair, trying to move quickly without making it worse than it already was. "I would like you to give me permission to alter a few of your dresses."

I saw her frown in the mirror. "My dresses?" she asked, her tone skeptical. "Why do you want to alter my dresses? Miss Blair swore it was in the latest fashion."

Ah. That cleared up a great deal of the situation. If a dressmaker failed to show her client to the best advantage and could not convince her client of the right cut, then she did not know her craft well enough. Miss Blair was, more than likely, new to the profession, and didn't think she was allowed to stand up to Mrs. Burnham, who loved bows and adornments far too much. Eugenia suffered because of it.

"The latest fashion, maybe," I said, trying to keep my tone kind. "But I think a different style would fit you better. Trust me, Miss Burnham, I know what I'm doing."

Anticipation made her eyes light up. "Oh, thank you, Nelson!" She twisted around in her chair and grabbed my hands. "Mary thinks you're the next best thing to a miracle worker."

Kind words from Mary? Had the world come to an end? "Well, I don't know about a miracle, but I will do what I can. Now, Miss Burnham, it's time for you to attend the opera."

"Yes, it is," Eugenia said with a wide smile. Her eyes were sparkling now, and she looked all the prettier for it. "I hear it's going to be a magnificent performance."

I raised an eyebrow as I stepped back, surprised by the statement. She had a fondness for music. Well, that was a first. I placed her cloak on her shoulders and tied it securely. "Enjoy your evening, Miss Burnham."

"I can't wait to hear what you plan to do," she said before she hurried out of her room.

Breathing out, I leaned against the small dressing table. I had a few hours to decide exactly what I could do for her. I couldn't disappoint her. Not when she was so excited to receive my help.

MISS GRAHAM CAME TO my room after the family left and the younger Burnham daughters were put to bed. "You made quite the impression on the girls," she commented, her voice failing to sound casual. "I didn't realize that you liked children, Juliet."

I looked up from the tiny desk that had been grudgingly provided for my use, where I was in the middle of composing a note. "I passed a few tolerable hours with them, and you assume that I like children? You should not make assumptions, Miss Graham."

"Well, I wouldn't have expected you even to tolerate them for a moment." The governess settled on the edge of my bed as had become her custom. "They wouldn't stop crowing about the time with you. Their talk nearly made me jealous."

That prompted a laugh from me, and I turned back to my message. "I'm glad you came," I said, changing the subject. "Could you have this delivered as soon as I'm finished? It would raise questions if I were to do so."

"Who is it for?"

Signing my name at the bottom, I blew on the ink to help it dry quicker. "I am arranging for Eugenia's hair to be cut. Mama's hairdresser is still in town, I believe, and he will be happy to help."

"You cannot cut Eugenia's hair!"

"I assure you I am not the one who will be doing the cutting," I said patiently as I sprinkled sand over the page so that the ink wouldn't smear when I folded the paper. "Heaven knows what the result would be if I even tried! No. Monsieur Lemaire will do so if he is available."

"Monsieur Lemaire? A Frenchman? Juliet, have you lost all your senses?"

"You cannot deny that when it comes to fashion and style, the French know their craft better than anyone," I said, with an amused smile. I didn't feel the need to explain that Monsieur Lemaire was merely an alias for a clever Englishman who knew to take an advantage when he could. "I would trust no one else to do this task."

Miss Graham shook her head. "Why must you cut her hair? Such long hair is admired."

"That may be, but you don't have to work with it." I folded the sheet of paper and scrawled Monsieur Lemaire's name across it. "It will be much more manageable once it is trimmed, and I believe it will compliment Eugenia's face. You'll see I'm right once it's done."

There was a skeptical look on her face when I glanced her way. "One of these days, you're going to learn you're not as clever as you think you are, Juliet," she warned, even as she took the message from my hand. "And something you decide to do will end in disaster. I just hope Eugenia isn't the victim when it happens."

I frowned at her. "Why do you say that? Nothing I've done so far has ended badly."

"That's exactly why I'm saying it. You're going to let it go to your head, and you will think you can get away with anything."

Her words gave me pause. "No, I don't think I will. I know I am not infallible, Miss Graham. I'm only human."

"It will, Juliet, because you are only human. All I ask is you remember Eugenia is a person, and not some doll, or chess piece, for you to play with and then throw away when you get bored."

"I would never do that!"

"But as soon as you think you have your own problem solved, and your family name redeemed, you will walk away," she said pointedly.

Dumbfounded, I stared at her. "Why are saying these things? You make me sound like a terrible person!"

Miss Graham sighed and raised her hand to her forehead. "You have given no thought to the consequences of your actions," she said, her words deliberate and careful. "Eugenia has faith you will help her attract Landon. Her heart is in this, and you will break it if you're not careful."

"What do you want me to say?" I asked in frustration. "I have been and will continue to be careful, Miss Graham. You know why I am here. I have a great deal to lose if I am not cautious in how I proceed."

"The reason you are here is the very thing I am concerned about. What happens once you learn what you wish to know? What will happen to Eugenia once you return to your proper place in society?"

While I hadn't thought that far in advance, I did know one thing: Eugenia was counting on me now. I would not be able to leave her without knowing she was going to be happy, and she had achieved what she most desired.

"I will not abandon something I've started. You have my word on that."

My former governess did not look even slightly satisfied with my answer. She pressed her lips together, before standing up. "I hope you know what you are doing." Fingers fluttered to her temple. "I find I have a headache."

My note to Monsieur Lemaire was still in her hand. "Can you add my letter to the post or should I see to it myself?"

She glanced down as though she'd forgotten what had started this whole disagreement. "I will. Good night, Juliet."

Turning, she left my room without another word. As I drummed my fingers on the desk, I frowned. The last thing I needed was another obstacle. I shook my head and stood up. Now was as good a time as any to see whether I could get into Mr. Burnham's office.

NO ONE WAS IN SIGHT as I approached the door. The rest of the staff were enjoying some time to themselves below stairs or handling any evening responsibilities. Would I find the office door locked?

The door handle didn't move when I tried to turn it. Without a key, I wasn't going to get in. "Are you looking for something, Miss Nelson?"

With a start, I pulled my hand back and turned to face Mr. Bridges. The man had an eyebrow raised. "I...had a question for Mr. Harper, and thought I would find him here," I said, thinking quickly. "Has he already left for the evening?"

Mr. Bridges' eyes narrowed. "I was not aware Mr. Harper had come today. Perhaps I can answer your question."

I waved my hand and backed away from the door. "Oh, no. It was not important. I wouldn't want to waste your time. Good evening, Mr. Bridges."

Swiftly, I walked towards the servants' staircase. I couldn't resist glancing over my shoulder. Mr. Bridges had the office door open and was entering. He closed the door and blocked my view.

My heart raced and it wasn't until I was in my room that I could start to relax. At least I had made the attempt. To calm myself, I decided to select the gowns I would alter for Eugenia. It would be easier without anyone looking over my shoulder to comment on what I should or shouldn't choose.

When I went down to Eugenia's room, I wasn't surprised to find Mary there. What I was shocked to see was a pile of gowns of all sorts on the bed. "Miss Eugenia said you wished to make adjustments to her wardrobe," the maid said nervously. "These are the colors that flatter her the most. I thought you might want to start with these."

"Thank you." I'd left Eugenia before she went down to join her mother. Mary must have spoken to her after I'd left. "I take it you agree with my plan?"

Mary raised an eyebrow. "At this point, I think anything will be an improvement for Miss Eugenia."

As long as we were on the same side for the moment, I could take the time to pass on the little words of wisdom Carter had bestowed on me. "A proper lady's maid must make sure her mistress looks her best," I said as I examined the garments. "To do otherwise would reflect badly on the maid."

"Then, why do you allow Mrs. Burnham to wear those shades of pink?"

Mary's expression of pure innocence didn't fool me. "Those pinks keep her happy, and I will not threaten Miss Burnham's peace by attempting to alter Mrs. Burnham's desires. I would be dismissed if I tried, and then where would Miss Burnham be?"

Leaving her to consider my words, I turned all my attention to the dresses. She had done an excellent job of selecting a variety for me to choose from. The lines of the dresses were well done, and the ostentatious adornments easy to remove. I made a point of informing Mary of my approval as I laid my selections over my arm. I took a morning dress and two evening gowns so I would have options for when Eugenia could present herself.

Was I getting ahead of myself, already planning for a presentation of Eugenia's improved appearance? Perhaps. Who knew if my appeal to Monsieur Lemaire would be answered. But I needed to believe everything would go well.

"If you tell me what needs else to be done, I can help," Mary said. "Two pairs of hands are better than one."

"I expect a message from someone who will be able to help with Miss Burnham's hair," I said, thinking through the plan I had. First, alter the dresses, then Eugenia's hair. "When it arrives, would you make sure it gets to me? Beyond that, I don't think there's much we can do until then."

"There's hope for her hair?"

The astonishment in her voice made me laugh. "Indeed there is. I will admit, the unruly nature of such thick hair puzzled me at first. However, I am consulting an expert on the matter. We will then have a better idea of how to proceed." I frowned at the gowns that were spread out on Eugenia's bed. "Shall I help you put the rest away?"

Mary waved a hand. "I'll take care of it, Miss Nelson. You have work to do, have you not?"

That had to be the first time she ever referred to me as 'Miss Nelson' and not sounded resentful about it. "Indeed I do. Thank you, Mary," I replied, with a smile. "If I should think of some way you can assist Miss Burnham in this project, I will let you know."

Feeling in charity with the everyone, I left the bedroom to return to my room and my sewing basket. I had significantly added to my workload, but I had every certainty it would all work out for the best.

"Miss Nelson, I believe."

Startled, I looked up. Oswyn Harper stood a few yards in front of me at the head of the stairs. Engrossed in my contemplations, I hadn't realized he was there. "Mr. Harper." I bobbed a respectful curtsey. "Mrs. Burnham and Miss Burnham are out."

"I am aware." He gazed at me in a perplexed way that made me uneasy.

Why was he here, yet again, when he had no right to be?

I couldn't question him, though, however much my curiosity burned to know all. If I didn't know better, I would have said he wished to court Eugenia. No doubt, if the ton knew how often he was in the house, there would be whispers he was doing just that, which would not be suitable for Eugenia if she wanted to catch Mr. Landon's eye.

"Excuse me, sir, I have work to do." I took a step forward to continue on my way. He didn't move from where he stood, blocking my path. "Is there something you require, sir?"

"I was curious about your references, Miss Nelson," he said, his gaze not moving from me. "Did you bring them with you when you first applied for the position?"

My references? I hadn't any references, but what was it Mrs. Burnham had said about references when I had been interviewed? "Why do you ask?"

"Let's call it curiosity."

Why was he suddenly so interested in me? What had I done to attract his attention? This was the last thing I needed to deal with now.

"I submitted my references when I first responded to the advertisement for the position," I informed him primly, pleased I remembered Mrs. Burnham mentioning this fact during my accidental interview with her. "You may ask Mrs. Burnham if you require confirmation."

He frowned, apparently not liking my response. "How strange," he murmured almost to himself. "You remind me of someone."

Oh, dear. I had to get away before he thought about it anymore.

"Mr. Harper, there you are. I've been expecting you."

I breathed a sigh of relief as Bridge stepped from Mr. Burnham's room. "Mr. Bridge," I said with a nod of my head.

The valet inclined his head in return, and Mr. Harper turned his attention towards him. Ducking my head, I took advantage of the distraction to hurry on my way. As I went down the stairs, I couldn't help glancing over my shoulder for one more look.

In doing so, I made eye contact with Mr. Harper. Feeling my cheeks burn with embarrassment, I looked away first and tried to keep from tripping over the dresses in my arms. I made my way as fast as I could to my bedroom, pressing my back against the door once I was safe inside.

Questions filled my mind. What were Mr. Harper and Bridges up to?

"I don't need another mystery to solve." I deposited my new project on the bed. As long as he did not try to interfere with my work, I would leave well enough alone.

At least, that's what I tried to convince myself I would do.

Chapter Ten

One of the things I dreaded most about my position was breaking my fast in Mrs. Wilder's sitting room.

Given how things had begun between the housekeeper and me, it was not a meal I relished, no matter how hungry I was. I would take my time leaving the family's part of the house. I knew as soon as I entered the servants' section, my resolve to be unaffected by her brusque manner would be put severely to the test.

The day after I'd made the first steps toward helping Eugenia, I knocked lightly on Mrs. Wilder's door, hoping she would already be going about her business. My heart sank when she bid me to enter, and I opened the door to the bright, cheerful room. "Good morning, Mrs. Wilder," I said, determined to be as polite as possible. "How are you today?"

The woman looked up from her desk. For the briefest second, she seemed surprised to see me. "You are early, Miss Nelson." She looked back down at the papers on her desk. Her statement puzzled me, for I thought I had arrived at the same time I usually did. However, before I could work on it any further, she asked, "How did you find the mistress and Miss Eugenia this morning?"

"Mrs. Burnham was exhausted from her activities last night and went back to sleep, and Miss Burnham seemed to be ready to face the day," I said, moving further into the small sitting room. I had made it a point not to sit down until invited, as a way of respecting her domain. "You appear to have a great deal to do, Mrs. Wilder."

"Not all of us have the leisure to rise so late in the morning." She waved a hand, a habit I had assumed she'd learned from Mrs. Burnham. "Sit down already. Mary will be bringing your tray in soon."

Taking a seat, I watched her at her work. In the hierarchy of the servants' hall, she would technically be above me, even though I did not come under her control. If I were to sway her opinion to at least look on me as—I couldn't think of the right term—maybe someone who was useful, perhaps the rest would follow. And my task would become much easier to complete.

"It looks as though we will have fine weather today."

The weather was a general enough topic I hoped would be the start of a conversation. However, it was a vain hope for I received no response. "You have served the Burnhams for many years, I presume?" Perhaps something closer to her own life would prompt an answer.

"I have."

Her short tone did not encourage conversation. But I knew I needed all the help from the other servants I could get. "You must know the family well then," I continued, stubbornly. "You've watched Miss Burnham grow up?"

Setting her pen down, Mrs. Wilder turned in her chair towards me. Finally, I had her attention. "Exactly what information do you wish to learn, Miss Nelson?" she asked, her tone bordering on hostile once again. "Do not think you can sweet talk anything out of me, or anyone else in the household."

"Mrs. Wilder, if I am to be of any help to Miss Burnham in attaining a good match, I simply must know more about her and her family." I raised my eyebrow. "Isn't that so?"

"And why would you be concerned about Miss Eugenia's matrimonial prospects? It has nothing to do with you."

I barely kept from sighing. Would I ever overcome her hostility? "Is it not the duty of any good lady's maid to encourage and aid her mistress? It is my responsibility to ensure she looks her best when she faces society. I have a plan I hoped you would be willing to assist me with."

Mrs. Wilder continued to stare at me, and it rattled my already unsteady nerves. The expression in her eyes had changed from dislike to slight puzzlement. At least, I had her attention. "You speak like an educated lady, Miss Nelson."

Startled by the blunt statement, I blinked. "I imagine I am not the only woman in service who has had an education," I said slowly, unsure of exactly what she meant by those words. Was it merely an observation or an accusation? "In fact, is it not encouraged for a maid to be clever?"

"Perhaps. But I do have to wonder why, all the sudden, so many questions are being asked in this household."

Before she could elaborate on that point, the door opened. Mary appeared, carrying a tray laden with food. She sent a conspiratorial look in my direction and then dropped her gaze to the tray as she set it in front of me.

A small, sealed letter lay next to the teapot. Monsieur Lemaire's response? I glanced over at the housekeeper, only to find she was once again occupied with her paperwork. "Thank you, Mary," I said, calmly.

Her lips twitched as though she wanted to smile, and then she hurried out of the room. Mrs. Wilder continued working, and I picked the letter up. Breaking the seal, I scanned the brief message informing me Monsieur Lemaire did indeed recall 'Madame Sinclair' and would be pleased to call upon Miss Burnham to offer his advice that very morning.

All at once fidgety from nerves, I devoured my meal. Mrs. Wilder lifted her head as I stood up. "No other questions, Miss Nelson?" she asked, raising an eyebrow. Her gaze was thoughtful, curious, and I felt vulnerable.

Where would I even start? "Actually..." I struggled to think and my courage failed me. "No, I don't think so. Have a good day, Mrs. Wilder. Perhaps we could continue our conversation later?"

She said nothing in response as I left the room. Once in the hallway, I breathed out a long sigh of relief. I needed her on my side, yes, but in no way could she suspect I was not who I said I was. How was I supposed to do that when she was a little too curious about me?

First of all, I would have to be a little more cautious about what I said and did. If I behaved like a proper lady's maid and kept my thoughts to myself, I should be able to escape any undue notice. And second...to be honest, I couldn't think of what my second step could be.

Shaking my head, I forced my feet to move. I had a job to do and a young lady to prepare. I would have to spend more time devising a plan to avoid Mrs. Wilder's scrutiny.

"WHAT IF NOTHING CAN be done?"

Laying out the evening gown I had worked into the night to finish, I barely kept from sighing. Eugenia had repeated that question for over an hour. The first dozen times I'd done my best to reassure her and Mary, who was just as nervous, but I was quickly reaching the limit of my patience.

"Losing hope will do none of us any good." Doing my best to soften my sharp tone, I turned to face the two younger women. "Monsieur Lemaire is a talented hairdresser, and he has been known to work miracles."

I regretted my sharp words as soon as I saw Eugenia's face twist in despair. "It will take more than a miracle to manage this mess," she said, waving a hand at her hair. I'd not attempted to tame it this morning, knowing it would be best for Monsieur Lemaire to see it at its worst. "I will never make Landon see me."

"He already sees you, Miss," Mary said, resting a comforting hand on Eugenia's shoulder. "Why, he stood up to dance with you twice at the last ball you attended. And did you not tell me he came to your opera box?"

Such actions showed Mr. Landon had at least a passing interest in her. "He was simply being polite," Eugenia said in protest. "He's not the only man who's danced with me twice in one evening, or called the day after."

"But he is the one you admire," I murmured, my heart reminding me it still felt some grief over losing Henry. As angry as I was with him and how he'd abandoned me when I'd needed him most, I'd truly loved him once, and I remembered well how it was to want his attention, to be noticed.

Neither of them overheard me, which was undoubtedly a good thing. "Well," I said, straightening my back. "If you don't want to do this, you should have told me before I finished your dress for this evening."

Eugenia admired the gown. "Oh, it looks so lovely, Nelson," she said, not having paid any attention when I had carried it into the room. She rose from her dressing table to inspect my handiwork. "I hardly recognize it. But, is it supposed to be so...simple?"

"Yes," I said emphatically. "One or two adornments are all very well in their place, when they are used with moderation and skill. But to have an abundance of lace, feathers, or beading will hide your slender figure and draws the wrong sort of attention."

"And no one will recognize this as a dress you've worn before, Miss," Mary added, her tone practical. "Once all your gowns have been altered, it will be as though you have a new wardrobe, without having to go through the time or expense of getting it."

Never mind it would need all of my time to make the alterations. But, Eugenia had been teased out of her worry, and I wasn't about to remind her of her uncertainties. In any event, the bedroom door opened, drawing all of our attention.

"There is a Monsieur Lemaire in the drawing room," Molly, the other maid, announced. Her tone was filled with curiosity. "He says Miss Burnham requested his attendance."

Eugenia's eyes widened and her face paled. "Oh...I...I..."

"Please show him up," I said since it seemed I would have to be the one to take charge. "He is expected."

With a nod, Molly hurried out. I swept the dress into the wardrobe, where it could stay out of the way and unharmed by any misfortune. Mary glanced at the door. "Mrs. Wilder will be wondering where I am. I should return to my duties."

"Oh, please don't go," Eugenia said, her tone pleading. "I need you here, Mary."

"Miss Burnham is correct." I was not about to be left to deal with Eugenia's nerves on my own. "If you are to know how to dress her hair when I am unavailable, you need to remain here. I will explain to Mrs. Wilder."

Mary's expression twisted into fear and apprehension. However, I didn't have the time to reassure her. I faced the door as it opened and a man stepped in. He was not as tall as I remembered, but his dark eyes had the same intelligent spark I remembered. "Monsieur," I said, dropping a respectful curtsey. "I am Miss Nelson. I sent you the message on Miss Burnham's behalf. Thank you for coming on such short notice."

As he nodded in acknowledgment, I noted he hadn't changed much in the five years since I'd last seen him. The beginning of grey in his dark hair made him appear even more distinguished. He still carried the same bag containing the instruments of his trade, and his mode of dress was as impeccable as it had ever been.

"Mademoiselle Nelson," he said with only slightest hint of a French accent in his voice. For a moment, his eyes met mine. There was a slight frown on his forehead and the flicker of recognition in his eyes that vanished as he turned to Eugenia. "It is indeed a great pleasure to meet you, at last, Mademoiselle Burnham. I've heard a great deal about your charm and sweetness."

I'd known there was a risk he would recognize me. After all, he'd cut my hair for my first Season in London. He'd also spent many years doing the same for my mother, who'd adored him, and who I'm told I resemble a great deal.

I could only hope I'd have the chance to extract a promise of secrecy from him before he left, and then pray he was still the same honorable man I'd known.

"Monsieur, I do hope you can help me," Eugenia said, sincerely. "I have done everything else possible."

I took up position beside Mary as the man went straight to work. First, he felt the texture of Eugenia's hair and tutted. "Have no fear, Mademoiselle," he said, his voice full of confidence. "I know exactly what must be done. If you would please have a seat? We must begin right away."

Eyes still as round as could be, Eugenia sat down. Setting his bag on the dressing table, Lemaire began to lay out what he would need. "You were wise to summon me," he said to no one in particular. "We must have Mademoiselle Burnham shining as soon as possible, oui? We cannot have a certain young gentleman kept waiting for too much longer."

I couldn't help but smile. He was as well-informed as he'd ever been in the past. "Exactly," I said.

Eugenia made a slightly confused sound in her throat. "Ah, Mademoiselle Burnham," Lemaire said with a broad smile. "I am well acquainted with Madame Landon, you know. She comprehends nothing of her son's interest, for she is incapable of looking beyond what is on the surface. Let us show her the pearl that is hidden beneath this unfortunate appearance."

A clip of his scissors and a lock of her hair fell to the floor. There was no turning back now!

I FOLLOWED LEMAIRE into the hallway, leaving Eugenia under Mary's care. "I thank you for your time and attention, Monsieur," I said as I walked with him towards the front door. "What you have managed is truly astonishing."

"What is astonishing, Miss Sinclair, is that I should find you in such a position."

His accent had vanished entirely. Pursing my lips at his brutally honest statement, I glanced at him. "There are some things in life beyond our control, Monsieur." There was such pity in his eyes I couldn't meet his gaze for longer than a moment. "Please promise you will say nothing of this to anyone."

"I shall carry this secret to my grave," he said. "But will you not tell me the whole of the story? Your dear mother was a valued acquaintance to me. You were on the verge of a good connection, last I remember. That you have fallen so far is incomprehensible."

"As I said, sometimes our path in life takes an unexpected turn, and we have to continue on, even if we do not know where it will lead."

We reached the bottom of the stairs, and Lemaire turned towards me. "Have no fear, my dear girl," he said, taking my hand. He bowed over it and then brought it up to his lips. "If you are ever in a position to need my services for yourself, I will put myself at your disposal."

Out of the corner of my eye, I saw Wilder glare at us. A hairdresser showing such respect to a maid? Unthinkable! I pulled my hand free of Lemaire's grasp. "Thank you, Monsieur." I remained in my place as the hairdresser left the house.

Wilder closed the door more firmly than was necessary and continued to glare at me.

Molly's voice came from the top of the stairs. "Miss Nelson, there you are," she said before the butler or I could say anything. "Mrs. Burnham has been demanding for you to come to her at once. She is furious you have not yet seen to her needs."

"And how long has she been asking for me?" I said, having a suspicion it had been some time.

The maid smirked. "It has been nearly an hour, Miss Nelson. You did say you weren't to be disturbed."

When had I said that? "Then, I should go smooth things over," I said, keeping my irritation out of my voice. Arguing with her would only waste my time and would no doubt make Mrs. Burnham even angrier, leading to my dismissal. I could, however, put my energy into appeasing my employer. "I'll make sure to mention your diligence in finding me, Molly."

Molly flinched. "I'm sure you will, Miss Nelson."

She spun on her heel and stalked away. Wilder made a slight huffing sound before he too left the foyer. I breathed out slowly and shook my head.

If it wasn't one thing, it was another.

Chapter Eleven

"You are finished here, Nelson."

Mrs. Burnham's sharp words greeted me as soon as I entered the room. She stood in the center of the room, her hands on her hips. Every response that came to mind were sarcastic and I suspected would not be appreciated. Holding my tongue, I went to the wardrobe. "Is there a particular gown you wish to wear tonight?"

My employer gave a dissatisfied huff as she sat at the dressing table. "The mauve silk," she said, her tone sullen. "You ought to have been here an hour ago, Nelson. What good are you if you are not available when I need you?"

With ease, I located the mauve gown. It was a new addition to Mrs. Burnham's wardrobe. "Miss Burnham required my assistance to prepare for tonight."

"I didn't ask for your excuses! Tomorrow, you will pack your bags and be gone."

I had the vague suspicion that this was how many lady's maids had found their employment ended. "Of course, Mrs. Burnham," I said calmly. I faced her, holding the selected gown. "I think you will look very well in this."

Twisting her head around, Mrs. Burnham stared at me over her shoulder. "I am serious, Nelson, and you will not leave with a reference from me."

Carefully laying the dress where it would be ready, I considered how to respond to this. I had not learned what I needed from the house, so I hardly wanted to leave. Otherwise, this whole masquerade was for nothing. How could I persuade Mrs. Burnham to change her mind, though?

"Perhaps you would prefer it if I were to leave immediately?"

At my question, Mrs. Burnham's eyes widened. It was a risky gamble, but one I had to try. She needed the services of a lady's maid. There was no doubt about that. It had taken her a great deal of time and effort to hire me, so it was not likely that there would be a quick replacement if I were to leave. We both knew this.

For a moment, anger burned in her eyes, and then she spun to face the mirror. "Get on with your work, Nelson!" she said sharply. "Eugenia and I are expected at the Gardners' for dinner."

Hiding a triumphant smile, I moved to begin arranging her hair. It took longer than usual to get Mrs. Burnham ready for the dinner party. She was sullen and dissatisfied with everything I did.

Finally, my employer was dressed and on her way down the stairs. I left the cleaning of the dressing room for later and rushed back to Eugenia's room. The young lady and Mary both turned to face me as I entered.

"How do I look?" Eugenia asked apprehensively.

Her once long brown hair had been cropped to only a few inches in length tapering even shorter to her neck. Now that it was no longer weighed down, Eugenia's locks had a distinct curl to them, and Monsieur Lemaire had shaped the cut masterfully. It drew attention to Eugenia's cheekbones, making her face appear longer and her eyes brighter.

Mary had woven a string of pale pink beads among the soft curls, which were brushed forward a la Titus as it was called. The white gown I'd altered looked elegant now it was free of its encumbrances, and it showed Eugenia's figure off to perfection. Her fan was clenched tightly in her gloved hands.

"Miss Burnham, you look splendid." Eugenia blushed from my praise. I went to her and gently pried her fingers from the death grip she had on her poor fan. "Mr. Landon will not know you when you arrive. The important question is, though, how do you think you look?"

She took a deep breath and faced the mirror again. "I think I look very well," she said, a note of surprise in her voice. She glanced over in a slight panic, though. "But what will Mama have to say about this?"

No doubt Mrs. Burnham would have a great deal to say on the subject. "Why don't you go down and find out, Miss Burnham?" I held the fan out to her.

Accepting the necessary accessory, Eugenia took a deep breath and nodded. She smoothed her white kid gloves one last time and then walked out of the bedroom. Mary and I exchanged glances and, without a word, we followed her out.

"Genie!"

"What happened to you?"

I cringed as two young voices made themselves heard. "Miss Daphne, Miss Calliope," I said sternly. "Am I to assume you have escaped Miss Graham's keeping once again?"

Calliope barely glanced at me as she circled her older sister, trying to get a good look at Eugenia's hair. "You look so different, Eugenia," Daphne said, tugging on the sleeve of her sister's dress. "Why didn't you tell us you were going to do this? What happened to all the feathers and lace?"

"I can't believe that Mama gave you permission to cut your hair!" Calliope said, her eyes wide. "Can I get my hair cut?"

"Eugenia!" Mrs. Burnham called, a note of real annoyance in her voice. "Any longer and we will not be able to attend."

"Daphne, Calliope, I have to go," Eugenia said, trying to escape her younger sisters' scrutiny. "Mama is angry that I have kept her waiting. Go back to Miss Graham, and I will tell you everything in the morning."

Daphne shook her head. "Ol' Gray Boots is not here. She said she had an important errand to run."

I frowned at that bit of news but set it aside in my mind until I had the time to deal with it appropriately. "That's enough!" I caught Daphne's hands and pulled her away from the dress I'd taken so much care with. "Even without your governess, I'm sure you can find some way of keeping yourself entertained, you cheeky gudgeons. Unless you need more socks to darn?"

The Shakespearean insult fell from my lips with an ease that should have alarmed me. Aunt Beth's habit had rubbed off on me without me realizing. My attention, though, was on Daphne and Calliope.

The subtle threat made both girls turn pale. They spun on their heels and bolted back the way they'd come. I sent an exasperated look towards Mary, but she was fussing with the dress, making sure no harm had come to it. Eugenia continued towards the landing, and I followed several steps behind.

"Eugenia!" Mrs. Burnham snapped, her gaze on her reticule as Eugenia descended the stairs. "We must be on our way."

"I'm ready, Mama," Eugenia said as she reached the bottom.

Mrs. Burnham finally looked up, and her jaw dropped. "Eugenia! What have you done?"

Concerned, I watched Eugenia twist her hands into the fabric of her gown. "Monsieur Lemaire cut my hair, Mama, so that it could be more easily managed, and Nelson altered my gown to be more the thing. I think it looks splendid, don't you?"

"Your hair, Eugenia!" Mrs. Burnham's voice rose several octaves, and I saw Eugenia wince. "Your long beautiful hair! Your dress!"

"Mama, it was not beautiful," Eugenia said patiently. "I am assured it will be much easier to manage now."

Shaking her head, as though she were denying the sight in front of her, Mrs. Burnham moved forward. "Where are the ribbons and beads? The gown is so plain and unremarkable now! The dressmaker insisted the embellishments would draw attention to you! Do you realize how much was spent on that dress?"

Why wasn't I surprised that she focused on Eugenia's gown? She wasn't wrong about the attention the dress might attract, but it wasn't the positive attention Eugenia needed, and I had to bite my lip to keep from intruding into the conversation. Beside me, Mary was wringing her hands anxiously. I reached over to rest a reassuring hand on her shoulder.

"Mama, I am pleased with the alterations Nelson has done. Come. The carriage is waiting."

"We cannot go with you looking like this! What would people say?"

"What will people say if we don't go?" her daughter countered with a surprising amount of determination. She began walking towards Wilder, who was holding the door open. "Mama, we must leave, or we will be late."

Her new appearance seemed to have infused Eugenia with confidence. Mrs. Burnham blinked and stared at her daughter a moment before rushing to catch up. "Eugenia, I am very angry with you."

Wilder closed the door behind her, and Mary breathed out a sigh of relief. "Mrs. Burnham will dismiss you for certain."

"No, I don't think she will," I said, pulling my hand back. Mary sent a puzzled look my way. "Well, if you consider what a difficult time she had in acquiring my services in the first place, I don't imagine she will be anxious to be rid of me so easily."

"Not even with me to take over again?"

Before I answered, I studied her face. There was no threat in the question, just open curiosity. "She did not consider you before," I said gently. "A few weeks will not have changed her opinion."

"I suppose you are right," she said as she turned from the stairs. "At this rate, I will never get ahead."

"Oh, you will," I said, falling into step beside her. "I will not be here forever, and I have every intention of making sure you are ready to fill my shoes when I take my leave. I expect it won't be long before Miss Burnham has accepted Mr. Landon's offer and she will need you when she is a married woman."

The maid frowned. "You seem to have everything worked out."

"It's easy to manage someone else's life," I said with a slight laugh. We reached the door to Mrs. Burnham's dressing room.

As I was about to push the door open, I paused. "Mary, how long has Mr. Harper been coming to the house?"

Surprised, Mary tilted her head. "Mr. Harper?" she repeated. "He's been assisting Mr. Burnham with his business for about five years now."

"What kind of business?"

Mary shrugged. "I have no idea, Miss Nelson. Bridges refuses to breathe a word about it, though he may have told Miss Graham," she added with a cheeky grin. It seemed I was the last to be aware of my former governess' affections. "She's the one you should ask."

"I'll do that."

"What exactly does 'cheeky gudgeons' mean?"

Shaking my head, I chuckled. "Honestly? I have no idea. My...former employer had a habit of using insults from Shakespeare's works on any and every occasion. I suppose I simply remember from that."

My response sent her off with a frown. I returned to the dressing room, closing the door behind me. My eyes felt tired and heavy. I allowed them a brief rest as I leaned against the door.

Five years. Was it a coincidence Mr. Harper was in the same place as the one person who knew why my father had come to London? And in the same year, my parents and brother had died?

"I wouldn't be surprised if he knows something I need to know," I said out loud. Sighing, I pushed myself upright. Somehow, I had to have a few words with Mr. Harper and try to get some information from him.

And Miss Graham. She was keeping more from me than I'd initially thought. Why was she continually leaving her charges for errands, and at this late hour?

MRS. BURNHAM WAS IN a much different frame of mind when she returned late that night. She raved about the stir that Eugenia had made at the dinner party, and how Landon had been unable to keep his eyes off of her. She ended with the triumphant statement that Landon had asked to take Eugenia driving the following day.

"And did Miss Burnham enjoy herself?" I asked, envying the fact that Mary would hear it all first hand from Eugenia.

"What does that matter? Landon is the most eligible gentleman to show any interest in Eugenia," Mrs. Burnham said dismissively. She rose from her dressing table and walked to her bed. "He's a younger son, to be sure, but my daughter would be lucky to have him and his five thousand a year. Or perhaps someone with more wealth will show an interest now she is more presentable."

It was fortunate her back was to me because I was sure I didn't keep my look of disgust from my face. I was certain Eugenia had a sincere interest in Landon, one that I hoped was reciprocated by the young man in question. Mrs. Burnham's mercenary viewpoint would most likely only lead Eugenia into heartache and sorrow.

But why was I even surprised? She'd already shown time and again that Eugenia's happiness was not the foremost concern in her mind.

"Will there be anything else, ma'am?" I asked, my tone sharper than it should have been.

She didn't seem to notice though. "No," she said, waving her hand in my general direction. She swept through the doorway into her bedroom, and I breathed out a sigh of relief.

Putting the dressing room to rights took only a few moments. I glanced in the direction of Eugenia's room when I stepped out into the hallway. A light flickered through the crack between the bottom of the door and the floor. No doubt she and Mary would be awake for some time.

A part of me wished I could join them, but I would only bring a damper to their excitement. As much as I yearned for it to be otherwise, I was not Eugenia's friend, and that was just the way it would have to be while I remained as a lady's maid. Julie Nelson could do much more for Eugenia than Juliet Sinclair could at the moment.

I would have to wait until the morning for a more sedate telling of how Eugenia's evening had been.

Yawning, I made my way to my room, having only the dim light of a single candle to guide my steps. I paused when I found my door slightly ajar. "Oh, not again. And here I thought everything was going so well," I said with a sigh. I pushed the door all the way open and stepped in to take stock of the damage.

On first glance, everything seemed untouched. Then the candlelight glinted on something on my pillow. Frowning, I stepped forward and bent down to have a closer look. My breath left my lips in a rush as I realized a slim pen knife was impaled in my pillow.

All trace of sleepiness was gone as I stared at the sight. My legs failed to keep me upright, and I fell to my knees by my bed. The destruction of Mrs. Burnham's dress had been malicious enough, but this? This was outright threatening.

I realized my hand was shaking dangerously and set my candle down before I set fire to my own bed. I then reached out to grasp the handle and pulled the knife free. It looked nothing like the same instruments I'd seen on the various desks in the Burnham house. In fact, it looked somewhat familiar. "Now where have I seen you before?" I asked, my curiosity taking priority over my fear.

Turning it over in my hand, I studied the knife. The dragon design suggested the owner was a man. Unable to place it, I laid it on the bedside table and sent a glance towards the door. The fact that there was no lock, and someone had been spiteful enough to leave a knife in my pillow, made me more than a little uneasy.

Swiftly, I pulled my chair and jammed the back of it under the doorknob. At least that would give me some warning if anyone tried to enter.

Not that I expected that to happen.

Well, I hoped it wouldn't happen.

Chapter Twelve

I felt as though I had reached a new level of tired when Mary roused me in the morning. When I heard the knock, I called out for her to come in. It wasn't until the door handle rattled and she declared that she couldn't get in, that I remembered the previous night, and surged to my feet in a panic.

Stumbling, I made it from my bed, pulled the chair free, and then opened the door. Holding the tray with my tea, the maid looked at me with a quizzical expression. "Sorry, Mary," I said, rubbing my hand across my eyes. "Please set it down at my table."

Mary carried the tray in. "Did you have a problem with Edward?" she asked, referring to the footman. "Is that why you blocked the door?"

"What? Oh, no." I stepped closer to my bedside table and picked the paper knife up. "Unless he has a habit of stabbing pillows."

"Stabbing—?" Mary repeated. She sent a glance at my pillow and saw the makeshift repair I'd done in the night. "Why would anyone do that?"

"Why would they destroy one of Mrs. Burnham's dresses?" I countered, raising my eyebrow at her.

An embarrassed blush stained her cheeks. "That is something else entirely," she said defensively, her tone flustered. She bent for a closer look at the opener and shook her head. "I've never seen that before. It's not from this house."

That declaration sent a chill through my heart. If it wasn't from the Burnham home, why did it look familiar? "Then where could it have come from?"

The maid shrugged and straightened up. "I honestly don't know. You should tell Mr. Wilder. If a person came into the house without anyone's knowledge, he needs to know that it happened."

"Of course," I said with a sigh. What Mary had said made sense, though I wasn't looking forward to the conversation with Wilder. Would he wonder why I was targeted? "I'll speak to him as soon as I'm dressed."

"Miss Eugenia wants to tell you about last night."

I wasn't surprised by that at all. I covered my mouth as I yawned and set the paper knife down. "Then, I will be down directly. Mrs. Burnham will not awaken for several more hours, I'm sure."

Mary nodded and left the room. Sighing, I sat on the edge of my bed and leaned my head back. I wanted more than anything to crawl back into the warmth of the blankets. After a few minutes of absolute silence, I forced myself onto my feet and went through my morning ablutions, moving slower than I'd ever done before.

As I reached for my cup of cooling tea I saw the letter. Picking it up, I did not immediately recognize the writing. Breaking the seal, I found a second letter enclosed inside. I pulled the first note and read it.

Miss Sinclair,

Mr. Bladen bribed one of the scullery maids to leave this letter in your room. However, I intercepted it. Kindly refrain from informing Miss Rycroft of this as I would very much dislike losing her trust.

Miss Carter

Henry Bladen had written to me? A glance at my watch told me that I didn't have the time to read it there and then, but I didn't dare leave either missive to be found by someone snooping. I tucked them both into my pocket and slipped the paper knife into my sewing basket.

Eugenia was up but not dressed, which was surprising considering Mary had already been there. She could not have slept for long, but only excitement showed on her face. "Have I something suitable for a drive in the park, Nelson?"

"Surely you know the contents of your own wardrobe, Miss Burnham," I said walking over to the sturdy piece of furniture. I flinched as I realized just how impertinent that sounded.

Fortunately, she didn't seem to notice. Falling back on her bed, Eugenia groaned. "But I have no carriage costume. I will look like a ninny."

"You are exaggerating things, and it does not become you," I said chidingly, glancing over my shoulder. I'd only had a brother, so to see the antics of a love struck young woman was both an amusing and irritating thing. "You know very well that a riding habit is not absolutely necessary to go driving with a gentleman."

As I spoke, I pulled a lovely pale blue walking gown from the wardrobe. I hadn't expected to need it so soon but it would only take a short time to be made acceptable. It was just the thing for a drive along Rotten Row.

"He told me I looked lovely last night," Eugenia said, sitting up. "All of the other guests were so complimentary about my new look, and everyone wanted to speak to me."

"Then they all seem to have good sense, which is more than I would have expected."

Tilting her head, Eugenia regarded me with a puzzled expression. "How did you know this would work, Nelson?"

The fact that I wasn't at all sure the changes would work was probably not something Eugenia needed to hear. "Is your mother going to be at home today, or will you have to accompany her on visits before Mr. Landon arrives?"

"I think we're staying at home today."

"Excellent," I said with some relief. "Then there will be no rushing about later on."

In no time at all, Eugenia was dressed in a morning gown. It too needed alteration but would be passable until I could alter the walking gown for her.

"I suppose I should go see my sisters before anyone comes to call," Eugenia said with resignation. "And Miss Graham has not yet seen my transformation."

I could only offer a smile in answer, remembering Miss Graham's scathing opinion of the whole thing. Eugenia left and I made quick work of tidying her room. There was some time before I needed to wake Mrs. Burnham so I returned to my room.

It was as I had left it, which was a relief. Now that Mary had suggested it, I knew I should report what had happened. I collected the paper knife and my pillow, the only evidence that my privacy had been invaded, and set off to find Wilder.

The lowest level of the house was bustling with the usual activity. I kept to the edge, first in the hallways and then in the kitchen, in an attempt to stay out of the way. My presence in the kitchen was noticed almost immediately.

"Miss Nelson." Edward, a tall footman, rose from his seat at the table. He was the one who had so impertinently winked at me on my first day. I had been thankful when he kept his distance after that. "What brings you to our part of the house?"

All movement came to a halt and everyone's gaze turned to me. "I must speak to Mr. Wilder." I knew I must look very odd, standing there with a pillow in my hands. "Where might I be able to find him at this hour?"

"Is there a problem, Miss Nelson?" a deep, disapproving voice asked from behind me.

With a start, I spun around to face the butler and I heard snickering from someone in the kitchen. "I have a matter to discuss with you in private," I said to him, stressing the final word.

Raising an eyebrow, Wilder nodded once and turned. Clutching the pillow to my chest, I followed him to his small office. Speculative whispers drifted after us as we walked, only being silenced when the door was firmly closed behind me.

"What seems to be the problem?"

I set my damaged pillow on his desk and drew the knife from my pocket. "When I went to my room to turn in for the night, I discovered that someone had left a rather unpleasant surprise: this knife in my pillow. The late hour kept me from informing you at the time, but I wanted you to be aware of what had happened."

"And you believe someone from this household did this?" he asked, a note of disbelief obvious in his voice.

"I didn't say that, and I do not believe it to be the case." I held the blade out to him. "Mary does not believe she has ever seen this paper knife within this house. She was appalled when I showed her."

For the first time, concern appeared on his face and he took the blade from me. "She is correct," he said, studying the item carefully. "I have never seen this design in this house."

Knowing that a person had entered my room was unsettling enough, but that it was someone not belonging to the house made it all the more terrifying. Why would they have done so? What purpose would it serve beyond frightening me?

Was the aim to frighten me into leaving the Burnhams' house?

"How am I to know this isn't an elaborate prank on your part, Miss Nelson?"

At Mr. Wilder's suspicious question, I drew myself up to my highest height, which wasn't all that impressive. "I have no need to embarrass either myself or you with such an action," I said unable to keep the haughtiness from my tone. "I am here to look out for Miss Burnham's wellbeing. Causing trouble would not be helpful to that end."

The corner of his lips quirked, as though he were fighting amusement. Then, he was all seriousness. "I will make inquiries of the staff. All the doors were locked once the family returned last night, and I did not detect any signs of a break-in this morning."

Well, that was hardly encouraging. "I will leave it in your capable hands," I said to him, picking up my pillow. "Good day."

"You've done a fine thing for Miss Eugenia," he commented as I began to turn. "And Mary speaks well of you."

I glanced over my shoulder. "Thank you," was all I could say to that. As an embarrassed blush heated my cheeks, I hurried out. I spotted Molly peeking around a doorway before she ducked back out of sight.

"Miss Nelson, will you be taking your breakfast now?" Mrs. Wilder asked, striding towards me. "Molly will return your pillow to your room."

Not exactly the solution I wanted given the damage I suspected the maid had done in my room before. However, Mrs. Wilder had never been so solicitous of me before, and I had no desire to cause any contention. "Of course, Mrs. Wilder."

"Molly, don't think I didn't see you hiding and eavesdropping," the housekeeper called out. She took my pillow, raising an eyebrow at the makeshift repair, as the maid stepped into view. "Molly, please replace Miss Nelson's pillow from the linen closet."

"There's no need for that!" I protested in surprise.

Mrs. Wilder held up her right hand, cutting me off, while offering my pillow to the maid with her other hand. "See to it, Molly."

Hanging her head, Molly scurried forward, grabbed the pillow, and then hurried off. "I'm afraid I have an urgent matter to resolve with the cook, and will not be able to join you," Mrs. Wilder said to me. "Mary will inform you when Mrs. Burnham has called for you. Good day, Miss Nelson."

Left with the housekeeper's room to myself? Shaking my head at the sudden change of attitude, I went to the room. A tray with tea and toast for my breakfast were waiting for me there.

It was then that I withdrew Henry Bladen's letter from my pocket. I broke the seal and carefully unfolded the paper. Sipping my tea, I leaned back to read what my almost-betrothed had written to me.

My dear Miss Sinclair,

Perhaps it is not the most proper thing for me to be writing to you, but I feel compelled to reveal the truth. Since our paths have crossed, I have not been able to stop thinking of you and remembering everything we went through so many years ago.

You must believe me when I say that it was not my choice to abandon you. I have never forgiven myself for the hurt my desertion must have caused. I tried to convince myself that you would be better off without me. It was the biggest mistake I have ever made, and I realized it too late.

Cowardice kept me from returning to you, dear Juliet. But now fate has seen fit to put you once more into my life...

My hands crumpled the letter before I finished. Tears had blurred my vision and I strove to blink them away. The anguish he had wrought returned anew, and I fought to push it back to the corner of my heart where it had been locked.

Slowly, the grief shifted into anger. "How dare he?" I said aloud, not recognizing my own voice. "How dare he!"

Did he honestly think that all it would take was an apology and all would be well? That I would accept his attention once again? Was he of the opinion that five years had done nothing to change me as a person?

Breathing out slowly, I smoothed the paper out. But instead of continuing to read, I folded it and slipped it back into my pocket. I did not have the patience to deal with his protestations. Perhaps I never would finish reading it.

I had just taken the last bite of my breakfast when Mary hurried in. "Mrs. Burnham is awake, Miss Nelson." She paused, a concerned expression appearing on her face. "Miss Nelson, are you well?"

"I am fine," I said, standing up. "Thank you, Mary."

She frowned but didn't say anymore. I resolved to forget about Henry's letter as I hurried up the stairs.

MRS. BURNHAM WAS SURPRISINGLY easy to satisfy. She was eager to greet visitors and, no doubt, extol the virtues of her dear Eugenia. Hints about courtship with Mr. Landon would no doubt be dropped in conversation as well.

How much I appreciated that my own mother hadn't been like that. Other ladies had sought some new kernel of gossip about Henry and myself each time they visited. But I had never had a cause for embarrassment from my mother. She allowed me my privacy, and I don't think I ever thanked her properly.

Before too long, it was time for Eugenia to dress for her drive. She was nervous and fidgety as I helped her into the walking dress, but when Molly appeared with the message that Mr. Landon had arrived, the change was immediate. Eugenia thanked the maid, looped her reticule strings around her wrist, and walked with sedate grace to the entrance hall.

I trailed along behind to make sure she didn't lose confidence and saw Gerard Landon for the first time since my own season. There could be no doubt that he really was a handsome young man, with dark brown hair, almost black, and blue eyes.

The way he smiled at Eugenia as he held out his arm told me a great deal about how he really felt.

Together, they made for a striking couple. I couldn't help a sigh of contentment as I watched them walk out of the house, arm in arm. Young love was a beautiful thing to behold, and I had every certainty that this romance would flourish.

Unlike my own.

Mr. Wilder closed the door behind them and sent an almost fatherly smile in my direction. I nodded in acknowledgment before I returned to my work. With Eugenia's courtship well on its way, I could finally focus on the main reason I had come to the Burnham house: clearing my family's name.

And I still had no idea how exactly I was going to do that with Mr. Burnham away.

Chapter Thirteen

Two days later, while altering Eugenia's wardrobe, I was pulled away from my work by an urgent message. I was wanted in the library. When I arrived, Mrs. Burnham was frowning at a letter in her hands. "Is there a problem, ma'am?" I asked when she didn't say anything for a long minute.

She barely glanced up. I suspected she had already begun advertising for a maid to replace me. I'd hoped once she saw how well Eugenia looked with her new hairstyle, she would forgive me for my impertinence. It hadn't happened.

"My husband will be returning at the end of the week," she said, a cool note in her voice. She didn't sound pleased or unhappy, just matter of fact. "There will be a great deal for you and the rest of the staff to do before he arrives."

Me? A great deal for me to do? My mind immediately went to the amount of work still left for Eugenia's wardrobe. If I had any hope of getting all the gowns done, all my time would be needed. How much household work would be expected of a lady's maid?

"I will bring Mrs. Wilder up to confer with you," I said, slowly. It was a surprise that the housekeeper hadn't been summoned along with me. Unless Mrs. Burnham wanted to drive a further wedge between the rest of the staff and me by making me her messenger. "I shall, of course, manage my responsibilities as expected."

"I am certain that Landon will be requesting an interview with Mr. Burnham very soon," my employer informed me, folding her letter. She placed the missive on top of the desk. "You must ensure that Eugenia keeps his attention until he has proposed to her."

There was much I wanted to say in response to her comment, but I held my tongue. I was getting good at that.

"Bridges will be pleased to have Mr. Burnham back, I'm sure." That was something I'd been wondering about. "How strange that Mr. Burnham went away for so long without his valet."

The older woman grimaced as she leaned back in her seat. "It is an odd habit he's developed these past five years," she said, sounding petulant. "Nothing I say on the matter will convince him that such an action is just not done. He does as he pleases and cares not that it vexes me greatly."

An odd habit indeed! Though I recalled that my father had traveled to London without a valet that last fatal journey he'd made to London. Was there a connection? So many things were pointing back to the year my parents died!

"Well don't just stand there, Nelson! Did I not just say there was much to be done?"

Pulled from my thoughts, I nodded. I suppose I should be grateful I had gotten away with as much impertinence as I had. "Of course. I will locate Mrs. Wilder for you immediately."

I made my escape without further hesitation. The news of Mr. Burnham's return was welcome. Finally, I would be able to meet the one person who could clear my family's name, and perhaps grant my family some closure, if he was willing to favor me with an explanation for my father's actions five years ago.

"You look pleased."

Bridges' voice startled me, and I looked up to find him only a few feet away. "Good news, Bridges," I said, determined not to let him see me flustered. "Mr. Burnham is to return."

An expression I couldn't quite identify crossed the valet's face. "Is he?" he asked. "This is a certain thing?"

"So Mrs. Burnham tells me."

He looked decidedly pleased then. "Then, I shall see to it that his chambers are in order. Thank you for informing me, Miss Nelson."

The way he said 'Nelson,' almost as though he were mocking me, sent a chill down my back. I was relieved that he turned and hurried away in the opposite direction. Puzzling over the valet's strange behavior, I made my way down to Mrs. Wilder's room. The door was open, and she was in conversation with the cook.

I cleared my throat to attract her attention. "Excuse me, Mrs. Wilder. Mrs. Burnham wishes to speak to you in the library."

The two women exchanged quick looks. "For what reason?" Mrs. Wilder asked.

Always there was that slight disrespect where Mrs. Burnham was concerned. Perhaps that accounted for some of the hostility that was directed at me. I wondered why they chose to stay in the house when they disliked their mistress so much.

"Mr. Burnham is to return at the end of the week. We must make the necessary arrangements."

The change in their attitude was instantaneous and answered my question about who they were loyal to and why they stayed. "I must plan the master's favorite meals," the cook declared standing up. "No doubt he will have been suffering from inferior dishes."

"Wilder will ensure the best wine will be ready to complement the meal," the housekeeper assured her, also rising. "We don't have much time to get this house shining."

Their restrained enthusiasm was astonishing. "May I ask something?" They both turned to me, with slightly impatient expressions on their faces. "Do either of you know why Mr. Burnham would go on a journey without Bridges? It seems strange that a gentleman would travel without the comfort of his valet."

"We've often wondered the same thing, Miss Nelson," Mrs. Wilder admitted. "No one can seem to find an explanation for it. Bridges certainly won't say a word on the matter."

Not wanting to keep them from their work, I nodded and left the room. Once I returned to my room, I picked up the dress I'd been working on, determined to get as much done as I could.

Where before I'd only had idle thoughts of Eugenia's growing happiness to consider, now I had the imminent return of Mr. Burnham to occupy my mind. I could finally learn something and perhaps put this farce to an end.

But the thought of returning to my aunt in Fairfield House did not hold the delight it once had. To go back to the monotony of having only my aunt's company seemed a bleak future. For as dearly as I loved Aunt Beth, I could foresee no alteration in my circumstances.

"But I will have peace of mind," I reminded myself, speaking softly. I smoothed the soft fabric beneath my fingers and shook my head. Once I knew the truth of the matter and had my family's good name restored, I could be content with life.

FOUR DAYS WERE ONES of non-stop activity for the household in general. Mary was kept from Eugenia's side the entire time, which was a sore point for them both. I wasn't delighted by the turn of events either, as it meant I was the sole person to calm Eugenia's nerves about Landon's increasingly frequent visits; a difficult feat when I also had Mrs. Burnham to satisfy at the same time.

Through it all, I kept watching for an opportunity to speak to Mr. Harper. Oddly enough, though, there was no sign of the young man in the house. Before he had been practically around every corner, but now when I wished for him, he was nowhere to be found.

It was vexing, to say the least.

Wilder said nothing more about the knife in my pillow. My belongings remained untouched in my room during the day. I kept my chair wedged firmly under my doorknob every night, for my peace of mind.

At some point in the mad chaos of preparations, I'd moved my workspace downstairs to the table in the servant's hall. It seemed more natural to be closer to the other staff than to take up their time having to summon me from my room.

Molly glared at me every time she hurried past. Mary would always pause to see what I had done, and I would take the opportunity to counsel her on the styles that would most flatter Eugenia. Cook unbent enough to keep the tea flowing whenever I was near the kitchen. The footmen attempted to become more friendly, but Wilder discouraged that straight away.

So when Molly came running with the news that Mr. Burnham's carriage had just pulled up, I was sitting at the kitchen table, having tea with the cook and Mary. Everyone was on their feet before I could even comprehend what the sudden fuss was about. I stayed where I was as Mrs. Wilder snapped out quick orders.

Molly and Mary were sent to unpack the master's trunks, which the footmen were dispatched to carry up. Cook began to boil a fresh pot of water sure that tea would be called for.

Folding my work, I stored it in my basket and rose to my feet. No one seemed to notice when I left the room. I carried the basket up to my room then hurried back down to the dressing room.

"There you are, Nelson! Why are you never here when I need you? Hurry! My husband has arrived, and I must go down to greet him. Why did you put me in this awful dress?"

Pointing out that she had insisted on wearing that particular dress would have been a waste of my breath. She was changed, and out of the room in the fastest time I'd ever managed. Maybe she was eager to see her husband after so long, but she'd never shown such eagerness before.

I really couldn't understand her.

The sound of running footsteps passed the door, accompanied by the familiar arguing of Calliope and Daphne. Stepping into the hallway in time to see the pair vanish down the stairs,

I shook my head. From their breathless excitement, there could be no doubt who was their favorite parent.

"Amusing children, aren't they?"

"That is one word for it, Mr. Bridges," I said, unable to keep from flinching. The valet stood in the hallway. The man had a talent for moving silently that I was beginning to detest. "Should you not be overseeing the unpacking of Mr. Burnham's trunks?"

The man smiled, but it wasn't a friendly smile. "Molly and Mary are handling the task well enough. You've not met Mr. Burnham have you, Miss Nelson?"

I opened my mouth to agree, but Miss Graham spoke up before I could say a word. "I don't suppose either of you has seen those two rapscallion charges of mine?" she asked. "I turn my back for one moment, and off they go."

"I believe they have gone down to greet their father, Miss Graham," I informed her, grateful for her presence. Bridges' intense stare was unnerving. "I don't think you're going to be able to pry them away."

The governess heaved a sigh, her eyes on the valet. "I suppose I will have to occupy my time some other way, then."

My cheeks flushed with embarrassment as I realized her suggestion was aimed at Bridges. When had Miss Graham become so forward and bold? She would have scolded me from dawn to dusk if she'd ever caught me implying such a thing!

"Excuse me," Bridges said. "I believe I am needed in the master's rooms."

"Poor Bridges," Miss Graham said with a sigh as her eyes followed him down the corridor. She moved closer to my side. "He's going to be so busy now."

"Yes, the reprieve from his duties is over," I agreed with little sympathy. "It's not every valet who is fortunate enough to have a master leave him behind every time he goes on a journey."

Miss Graham frowned at me. "Juliet, there is no call to be so disdainful of Bridges. Just because you've decided to play out this farce doesn't mean that you can make fun of those who have to support themselves with such work."

"I wasn't making fun of him, Miss Graham," I said, lowering my voice. The last thing I wanted was to be overheard. "And you know why I'm doing this."

"Well, now Mr. Burnham has returned, you can end this travesty," my former governess said, a sharp edge to her voice. "And then you can leave."

"Do you want to get rid of me?"

"Excuse me, Miss Nelson," Miss Graham said abruptly. "I have work to do, as I'm sure you do as well."

She walked past me, towards the staircase. I twisted to watch her go, puzzled by the change in her demeanor. I'd known she wasn't pleased with my decision to take the position, but she seemed outright angry with me now.

Why now; when I was so close to finding answers?

Shaking my head, I forced myself to move on. I had to plan how I was going to meet with Mr. Burnham.

THE RE WAS NO PLANNING necessary, as it turned out. Eugenia and Mrs. Burnham went to the opera, accompanied by Mr. Landon. As I cleaned up the dressing room, wondering how it could get in such disarray when I tried so hard to keep it organized, Mary appeared at the door. Mr. Burnham wished to speak to me.

The time had finally come. I took a deep breath and smoothed my dress. "There's no need to be nervous," Mary assured me. "I'm sure Mr. Burnham just wants to meet you. He's always careful about the staff and who stays."

"Mrs. Burnham has no doubt been complaining about my impertinent ways."

The expression on Mary's face changed to one of apprehension. "Mr. Burnham has always been fair," she said, her optimism waning slightly.

Forcing a smile, I nodded. As I made my way down to the library, I ran through my list of questions. Why had my parents come to London after my brother died? Why would someone try to implicate my family as traitors?

When I reached the door, I felt a moment of uncertainty. I couldn't remember if this was an instance where a servant would knock before they entered or not. Taking a chance, and hoping I was making the right choice, I grasped the doorknob, pushed the door open, and stepped into the room where my journey as a lady's maid had begun.

"You must be Nelson." Mr. Burnham looked up from his newspaper. He gestured to the space in front of his desk. "Please come in."

Swallowing hard, I walked to the chair and stood behind it. Mr. Burnham took the time to arrange his newspaper neatly, giving me an opportunity to study him. Since the last time I'd seen him, his hair had gone completely gray, and his face had lines that hadn't been there before. It made me a bit sad that such a kind, energetic man should show the years on his face.

"I'm told I have you to thank for Eugenia's transformation."

I folded my hands on the back of the chair and nodded. "Yes, sir." There was no change in his expression, and I had no idea what he thought about the dramatic change in Eugenia's appearance.

"My wife is displeased with you."

"I am aware of that, sir." What else could I say? I wasn't sorry for what I had done; Eugenia was the only one who mattered in this situation. "If given the opportunity, I would do it all over again."

My tone had come out more belligerent than I'd meant, and I inwardly cringed. Mr. Burnham frowned at me. "I didn't intend to berate you for this. I wanted to thank you. My daughter has never looked so well, or behaved in such a confident manner."

Everything I had been ready to say in defense of my actions vanished from my mind. "I am...pleased I could help Miss Burnham," I said slowly. "She deserves all the happiness in the world."

The man behind the desk gave a fond smile. "I will not argue with you there," he said as he stood up. "I simply wanted to thank you personally. You know I cannot guarantee that you will regain my wife's good opinion, but I can at least ensure you are provided with a favorable reference if you are dismissed."

"I could not ask for more than that." Not that my life would be at all affected by that reference. Once I left the Burnham house, I would not need to take another position as a lady's maid. "Thank you, sir. I was afraid I had offended Mr. Harper."

Mr. Burnham's eyes narrowed. "Mr. Harper? What has Mr. Harper to do with anything?"

"I don't know," I said slowly. "He's been here so often. I thought at first that he was courting Miss Burnham. I'm afraid I was not as cordial as I ought to have been."

"Harper? Here?"

I nodded. "Many times." A part of me felt guilty about revealing Harper's actions without having had the opportunity to ask him about it first. "And all over the house. I assumed you had given him free reign since he works with you."

From the expression on Mr. Burnham's face, I knew that wasn't the case. "No," he said, his tone short. He made to move around his desk, and I knew he would end our conversation. I couldn't lose my chance!

"Mr. Burnham, I do have a question, if I might have a few more moments of your time."

Surprised, he paused. "Oh? And what might that question be?"

"What can you tell me about the Sinclair family?"

Chapter Fourteen

I hadn't meant to blurt the question out so abruptly, and I immediately knew I had overstepped my bounds. Mr. Burnham's expression lost all traces of kindliness. "Forgive me, sir," I said swiftly, hoping desperately to cover over my blunder. I braced myself for the reprimand I knew was coming my way.

"Why would someone like you ask about the Sinclair family?" His tone was harsh, almost furious. "What do you know?"

"I—I knew the family, sir! I meant nothing by it."

After a moment, the tension on his face eased. "Ah yes. I recall my wife mentioning something about you having served the Sinclair household." My fingers tightened on the chair back as I managed a nod. "Is there a reason for asking that particular question?"

"Miss Juliet Sinclair is justifiably distressed by the recent rumor that has come out in the Times." How strange it was to speak of myself in the third person. "You haven't heard it?"

His eyes narrowed slightly, and he studied me with more interest than before. "And how, exactly, do you know what Miss Sinclair is distressed about? It hardly seems to be a matter for you to concern yourself with."

There, at least, I had a ready response. "You must know how intimate a lady is with her maid. Her circumstances may not allow for her to employ a maid now, but I have been kept apprised of what has happened in her life." Nothing of what I said was a lie but was misdirection. "Miss Sinclair is extremely distraught by the rumors that have been hinted at in the papers."

Mr. Burnham frowned, and then he heaved a sigh. "I heard something about it before I left London. I did not think anyone would take it seriously."

"Perhaps not, but Miss Sinclair has questions about what brought her parents to London five years ago. You must admit, it is strange that they would do so when they were in mourning for John—the young Mr. Sinclair."

I knew I'd made a mistake when I began to say 'Jonathan.' A maid wouldn't refer to the son of the family in such an informal way; not without there being an inappropriate connection between them. The faint hope that I had covered my error was shattered when Mr. Burnham's frown deepened.

"That is true," he agreed, his eyes studying me. "Tell me, Miss Nelson, have we met before? There is something familiar about your face."

My breath caught in my throat. "I am only a servant, sir, and even had our paths crossed, I doubt you would have reason to remember a lady's maid," I said vaguely.

I doubted he heard what I said when his eyes lit up. "In fact, you remind me of Sinclair." My hand flew to my mouth. "I won't embarrass you, Miss Nelson. I'm sure he wasn't the only man who fathered children outside his marriage, although I always assumed him to have been happy with his family life."

It took me a long moment to realize what he was saying, and then my cheeks heated up with a blush. "Oh, no," I protested. My father had been faithful to Mother! Of this I was certain!

Mr. Burnham held up his hand. "We will not speak of it anymore," he said, his tone becoming kind. "I am not in a position to judge, and no one shall hear of this from me, Miss Nelson."

Maybe it was best he made such an outrageous assumption. Juliet Sinclair would never be attached to this whole thing, and my reputation would be secure. Goodness, it was getting hard to keep each identity straight in my head!

"So, what can you tell me?" I prompted, eager to move on from the matter of my supposed illegitimacy. "Miss Sinclair's distress weighs on my mind, and I wish to give her some news if I can."

He shook his head, a strange kind of sadness creeping into his eyes. "Your loyalty to the lady does you some credit, but I have nothing to tell you."

Nothing? Somehow, I didn't believe that. I couldn't believe everything I had been through would bring me no information. "Then, if there is nothing you can tell, is there anything you can do to dispel these rumors for her?"

Again, I had pressed too hard. "If I had anything to tell, I would speak to the lady herself and not an impertinent maid who needs to learn her place." Mr. Burnham turned his attention to his papers, effectively dismissing me.

Taking a deep breath, I forced myself to make the necessary curtsy and withdrew from the room. As I hurried up to my room, I mentally chastised myself. If I'd approached him better— confessed who I really was, perhaps—would he have been more forthcoming?

In the end, he hadn't given any indication whether he would combat the rumors or not.

"It was all for nothing."

Sitting at the tiny dressing table in my room, I caught a look at my reflection. Dark shadows were under my eyes, hinting at the lack of sleep. Shifting my gaze to my hands, I studied the roughness of my skin, consequences of having to launder Mrs. Burnham's delicate articles of clothing.

So many hours of hard work! So many hours of lost sleep. And for what? To learn the gentleman I'd hoped to dispel the rumors could not–or would not–do anything to stop them.

"Stupid, stupid, stupid," I whispered, blinking away tears. I rubbed my fingers together, feeling the calluses that had built up on my fingertips from the alterations to Eugenia's gowns.

Eugenia. How well she looked and not merely because of the changes in her apparel. She was more confident in herself, and it showed in the way she carried herself.

So, no, my coming to the Burnham house had not been for nothing.

Lifting my gaze, I stared at myself in the mirror. "It's time to go home."

MY CONSCIENCE WOULDN'T allow me to pack up my meager belongings and leave. Mary was not quite ready for me to leave her with the responsibility of caring for Eugenia. She would fail immediately, and would no doubt lose any chance of advancing in the household.

Subtly, I began to show the maid some of the tricks I had learned from my great-aunt's maid. She had to know the latest fashions, and whether they would suit her mistress. Also, how to clean silk properly, which I had found very useful. I would equip Mary to take on a challenging position as much as I was able.

Four days after my somewhat disastrous discussion with Mr. Burnham, a full letter arrived from Aunt Beth's household. Fortunately, Eugenia and her mother were calling on friends, so there was nothing to keep me from opening the message immediately.

I ignored the small note from my aunt, guessing it contained more pleadings for me to return home, and instead focused on the letter. I recognized Mr. Burnham's handwriting, and I broke the seal, eager to know what he had to say to me, Juliet Sinclair. My eyes moved swiftly over the words, moving over words of greetings and well wishes until I reached the important section:

Your father was a dear friend of mine. That I was unable to assist him when he came to me for help has weighed heavily on my mind, given what I've learned since then. At the time, I dismissed his concerns about his son's death as the desperate imaginings of a grieving father. When I heard of his sudden demise, I knew he'd had a reason for concern.

The report that young Jonathan died from fever was not entirely correct. He was not traveling with friends when he died. I cannot go into any details, but please be assured that he was acting on behalf of this country and did work that was of vital importance to our war efforts.

Shocked, I stared at the words on the paper. My brother had been an agent of the government? How long had he done so? It hurt to realize that my brother, someone I thought I'd known well, had been a stranger to me and that I hadn't been told this because I was a female.

And he hadn't been with friends. The one thing that had always comforted me was that I believed Jonathan had died with his friends near him. Father had told me Jonathan was buried quickly, near Bath, to prevent his illness from spreading.

Shaking my head, I tried to make sense of it all. Of course, my father must have known what Jonathan was doing. How else would Jonathan have had the money for his frequent travels?

How had he really died? Mr. Burnham said the fever 'was not quite true.' What did that mean? Confused, and hoping for answers, I read on.

Someone in league with Napoleon discovered Jonathan's identity and removed him from the situation. Your father came to me with concerns about the possibility that one of Jonathan's friends might have been that person.

One of Jonathan's friends? That news drew my focus back from my grief. It didn't make any sense. Remembering Jonathan's friends, those I had met before, I couldn't believe any of them would have hurt my brother...but look how little I'd truly known Jonathan.

"Oswyn Harper," I breathed, unable to think of anyone else. I already knew he had been working with Mr. Burnham for five years. What would have prevented him from copying information and passing it on? "But why would he do something like that?"

Obviously, a man who wanted the money would, for I could only imagine bringing such information to the other side would be well rewarded. Was Mr. Harper in a position where he needed money? Would he have betrayed my brother's friendship?

Confused and troubled by this, I refocused on the letter. There were only a few lines left.

Such news will no doubt distress you but have no fear for the future. With Napoleon captured and the war over, I have every faith justice will be done here in our country.

I regret I have not kept in contact with you, my dear Miss Sinclair. The rumors that have been circulating have no basis in truth, and I will endeavor to lay them to rest if I can. Rest assured that if there is any need, merely send word to me and I will assist you in any way I can.

Yours,

Burnham

If only he had responded before I'd embarked on my pretense of being a lady's maid! Which made me wonder if he had even received my letters before. Feeling shaken, I set the letter down, knowing I would have to destroy it or return it to Aunt Beth before anyone discovered it.

A small detail wouldn't leave my mind, and it prompted me to lift the letter once again to reread it. There it was: *When I heard of his sudden demise, I knew he'd had reason for concern.* My father's visit to London had been sudden, and now I knew why.

If my brother's death hadn't been an illness but as a result of some cruel man's deliberate actions, how would such a man react if the father of his victim behaved in a manner indicating suspicion? "He killed my parents," I breathed. "It wasn't an accident."

My family had been taken from me intentionally. Everything I thought I knew was wrong. My parents and brother had been murdered, and I had lived for five years without knowing the truth.

I had taken comfort from the fact that their deaths could not have been foreseen; a carriage accident and a sudden illness. The kind of occurrences that no one could control, and I could have done nothing to prevent. But murder?

How many people had known and hadn't told me? Uncle Frederick must have known, and he'd just gone off on his travels without a word to me of the truth. Had Aunt Beth known and just wanted to keep from hurting me?

But, what stung the most, was the revelation that I hadn't known my father or brother at all.

For four years, I'd laughed and joked with Jonathan, teased him about his love of travel. The whole time he'd been keeping such a huge secret from me. A small part of me knew that he'd done it to protect me from any danger that his missions would have brought, but I thought we'd been close. Now I would never have the opportunity to understand him because someone had ended his life far too soon, to keep him from passing vital information.

Even when they'd suspected Jonathan had been murdered, my parents hadn't told me. I could understand why Father would keep my brother's secret from me while he was alive, but why could I not know the truth when Jonathan was gone? Had Mother known?

Mr. Burnham's revelations had only brought more questions, and I couldn't make sense of any of it. Tears burned in my eyes and I collapsed onto my bed. I buried my face in the pillow in an attempt to keep from being heard.

I didn't know how long I cried before I sensed someone sitting on the bed beside me. "Miss Nelson," I heard Mary say, as she placed a comforting hand on my shoulder. "Miss Nelson, what's happened? What's wrong?"

Struggling to bring my emotions under control, I lifted my head. "It's nothing," I managed to say, wiping the tears from my cheeks. I must have looked a mess.

"I don't believe that," Mary said, pulling her hand back. Her dark blue eyes were filled with concern. "Have you been dismissed?"

"No, nothing like that." I sat up and ran my hand over my face more firmly. "I just...heard some bad news about my family."

"Do you want to talk about it?"

Shaking my head, I pulled my pillow closer and hugged it to my chest. "I can't. Not right now." I took a deep breath. "I think I should finish training you to take over my position, Mary. You know most of the work as it is."

"But I thought you weren't dismissed!"

"I'm not," I said, looking away. "But I can't stay much longer. It will be better if I leave on my own terms."

Mary shook her head. " Why would you leave? You have it good here."

That drew a short laugh from me. "With Mrs. Burnham? No, Mary. I think Mrs. Burnham is biding her time until Eugenia is married, and then she will happily turn me off. I'd rather take my chances and leave with a good record."

The maid frowned. "But what if I'm not allowed to take over?"

"I'm sure Eugenia wouldn't have it any other way," I told her. Why was it that reassuring others could so easily take my mind off my own worries? My grief had receded to a more manageable level. "In any event, whether I remain or not, you must prepare yourself to get ahead. Why not begin the training now?"

Bells ringing out the time could be heard, and Mary let out a gasp. "They'll be returning soon!" she exclaimed, scrambling to her feet. "I'll help you get everything ready and see to Miss Eugenia."

It was such a change from our first meeting, and the resentment she'd shown for so long.

"I appreciate it." I pushed myself to my feet and hurried to my basin. I splashed cold water on my face and then dried off. I followed Mary into the hallway, making sure to close my door behind me.

"Did Mr. Wilder have anything to say about the damage to your pillow?" Mary asked, over her shoulder.

"The knife didn't come from the house, and that was all he could tell me." In fact, I'd meant to ask him about it and simply hadn't had the time. "So, either someone here in the house got it from elsewhere, or...."

She paused and spun around. "An intruder? Why? Who would do such a thing? Someone who doesn't like you?"

I opened my mouth to refute her suggestion, but couldn't bring myself to deny it with any degree of certainty. What if the same person who had murdered my family had discovered I was looking for answers and wanted to stop me? "I don't know, Mary."

THANKS TO MARY'S HELP, I was in my bed early. Though my mind kept going around in circles, I did manage to get some sleep. A full night of uninterrupted rest did wonders to my frame of mind, and in the light of day, I was able to consider my next step.

There was little more I could learn in the Burnham house. Mr. Burnham's letter had told me all he could, and probably more than he should have. I would have to look elsewhere to discover more about the secrets my family had kept from me. And I knew exactly where I should go.

Bath. The last place my brother had been, and where he'd been murdered. If I could discover who he had been visiting and talking to when he was alive, I might find some clue to his murderer.

"And then what do you think you'll do with that kind of information?" I asked myself as I brushed my hair. I met my brown-eyed gaze in the mirror. "Bring the man to justice all by yourself?"

Shaking my head with a sigh, I began to twist my brown hair into a severe knot at the back of my head. I also needed to speak to Wilder about the knife that had been so considerately left in my pillow. Had he discovered its provenance, or who could have left it? If he hadn't learned anything, I wanted it back.

Again, I wished I could remember where I had seen it before. It would lead me closer to whoever felt so threatened by my presence in the household. As I was thinking about it, there was a sharp knock on my door. "I'll be there in a moment," I called, jamming pins into my hair. There came a second knock, even more insistent than before. "I said just a moment!"

For a third, time the person on the other side knocked. Frustrated, I stood up, hoping the pins would keep my hair in place long enough to get rid of my determined visitor. "I'm coming," I said, stalking over to the door. I jerked it open and gave a start at the sight of the tall young man who stood with his hand upraised to knock yet again. "Mr. Harper! What are you doing here?"

A door slammed nearby, startling us both. Mr. Harper glanced around, then grabbed my arms. I managed a squeak of protest as he pushed me back from the doorway so he could enter. He closed the door with his foot, then spun me around, pinning me against the door.

"You and I need to have a little talk, Miss Nelson."

Chapter Fifteen

Alarmed, I opened my mouth to protest the rough treatment. Mr. Harper clamped his hand over my mouth, cutting me off before I could even try. "I give you my word that I will not hurt you, but I need answers," he said. "And I would rather not have any interruptions."

How dare he enter my room and attack me like this? For a moment, I was furious, both with him and myself. Why had I not been more cautious in opening my door? Struggling to get free, I tried to kick his ankles, but his leather boots protected his ankles well enough that he just ignored my attack. He held me against the door with seemingly minimal effort.

Fear gripped me then, replacing my anger. The knife in my pillow had been a warning, after all, and I hadn't left the house. Was this attack the next step in ensuring I left the house? My heartbeat pounded in my ears.

"If you give me your word that you will not give me any trouble, I will release you." The calm way he spoke to me made him sound infuriatingly reasonable. "Please do not make this any more difficult than it has to be."

Breathing through my nose, I narrowed my eyes and glared at him. I would be as difficult as I very well pleased! How could he possibly think I would behave otherwise after being manhandled in such a rough manner?

"Do you really want to be discovered, alone in your room with a man, Miss Nelson?" His eyebrow echoed his question. "I imagine that would not reflect well on your otherwise impeccable record."

His face was only a few inches from mine. The only other man I had ever stood so close to was Henry Bladen, during our courtship. That thought made me go still, and he must have taken that for compliance because his grip on my arm loosened slightly. He didn't completely release me though.

"Will you keep quiet?"

What choice did I have? I nodded once, and he lifted his hand from my mouth. He gripped my other arm, clearly showing he didn't trust me not to struggle again. I took a deep breath and cleared my throat. "What do you want? Who do you think you are to come barging into my room like this?"

"I am the one with the questions," Harper said sharply. "I want to know who you're working for."

"Who I'm working for?" I repeated with a slight laugh. How had he guessed I had my reasons for being in the Burnham house? "I work for the Burnhams. And Mr. Burnham isn't going to like hearing how you barged into this room and attacked one of his employees. Now let me go."

"You pretend to work for the Burnhams, but I know you're here for another reason," Harper snapped. "Who are you passing information to?"

I gritted my teeth as I glared at him. His face was still close to mine, his breath brushing against my cheek. My gaze dropped to his mouth, and a highly improper idea came to mind. Before I could think better of it, I acted.

Closing my eyes and leaning forward, I pressed my lips against Oswyn Harper's.

Henry had kissed me several times in the months before my family died, and I had always enjoyed the experience. But this was completely different. Mr. Harper's lips were firm under mine, and he wasn't holding me in a remotely tender embrace.

My action seemed to startle him, and he loosened his grip on my arms. Reaching up, I put my hands on his chest and shoved as hard as I could. He stumbled back a few feet, drawing his hand over his mouth. Had it been any other situation, I might have been insulted at that. "What the—" he began to say.

I pushed away from the door, getting my breath back. "How dare you come in here and make such wild accusations? You're the one who has been in and out of this house while Mr. Burnham was away."

"I work with Mr. Burnham!" Harper said defensively. "I had business—"

"He knew nothing of you being in this house so often when I made mention of it. In fact, he seemed rather upset by the idea."

Mr. Harper blinked, and a frown began to form. "What? No, I had a message from him, asking that I keep my eyes on his household. That is what I was doing."

He looked so confident, and I began to feel the first stirrings of doubt. "He didn't say anything about that to me," I said uneasily. "So, it seems we have to work out which one of us is lying: you, me, or him."

"Burnham is an honorable man. He is not a liar."

"Neither am I." His gaze didn't waver even slightly from mine "But something tells me you're not lying either. One of us has to be."

The fingers of his right hand began to drum on the side of his leg. "I know there is a traitor in this house. It's possible that the person sent a fraudulent message to me to cause trouble." He narrowed his eyes. "Or you could be lying about what Burnham said to you."

I gave an unladylike snort. "Well, that wouldn't do me any good, would it? All you'll have to do is ask him, and how far could I get once you learned I'd lied?"

After a moment, he nodded to concede the fact. "That's true. Then again, it would be logical to suppose that Mr. Burnham had reason to tell you something that was not true."

He was stubbornly caught up on the idea that someone was prevaricating. "What reason would that be?" I demanded impatiently.

Harper raised his eyebrow. "Keeping you from the truth."

My first instinct was to scoff, but he did have a point. Had I been too eager to believe everything I had been told? "I suppose only time will tell."

"All of this doesn't explain what you're doing here, Miss Nelson."

Whenever he said 'Miss Nelson' there was the slightest hint of a sneer, as though he knew it wasn't my real name. "Helping Miss Burnham, of course." Before he could ask me any more questions, I asked one of my own, "What do you know about the Sinclair family?"

His eyes widened for a moment, betraying his surprise. "You're going to have to be a little more specific, Miss Nelson," he said, trying to sound nonchalant. "What about them?"

What was it Mr. Burnham had said? Someone who had been friends with Jonathan was likely the one who had killed him. Looking at Harper, standing right in front of me, I didn't think he looked like a killer. Then again, how would I know if I saw one?

I decided I may as well put some of my cards on the table, as it were. Thank you, Jonathan, for having taught me more card games than a lady should know how to play. "Did you kill Jonathan Sinclair?"

He gave a more obvious start in reaction to that question. "What? No!" He stepped forward and pointed at me. "Jonathan Sinclair was a good friend of mine, and I would have given my life in exchange for his."

Oddly enough, yet again, he sounded sincere. Maybe my instinct for the truth wasn't as accurate as I thought it was, but for the moment I decided to give him the benefit of the doubt. "So, you're aware he was murdered," I said, happy to have the advantage.

"How do you know?" he demanded in surprise. "That news is not public knowledge."

"You're right. Most people are under the impression that Jonathan Sinclair died of a fever he contracted in Bath." Never mind the fact that I'd been under the same impression not more than twelve hours before.

"You are remarkably well informed, Miss Nelson," Harper said with a frown. "How is it that you know so much?"

I could have told him the truth about who I was, but what reason did I have to trust him? He'd barged into my room and accused me of being a traitor. Until I could confirm exactly what part he played in the mess that had become my life, I needed to keep him at arm's length.

"Miss Sinclair," I said quietly.

A puzzled expression appeared on his face. "Miss Sinclair?" After a moment, I could see the understanding come in his eyes. "You mean Sinclair's sister? What about her? She doesn't have anything to with any of this."

"Oh, doesn't she? You don't think that she wants her brother's killer to be brought to justice?" I hissed. "The Sinclair family name has been dragged through the mud these past few months. You think that doesn't affect her?"

"You're remarkably protective," Harper said. "But then, you must be around the same age as Miss Sinclair and Mrs. Burnham did say you'd worked for the family. Did she send you here?" That was one way of putting it. I looked away. "What does it matter to her now? No doubt she is happily married. She was practically engaged five years ago. Sinclair told me."

I clenched my jaw at that and resisted the desire to slap him. "Oh, what do you know about it?" I put my hand on the doorknob. "And I'll ask you to leave my room now, sir. We can have nothing more to say to each other."

"Oh, I think there's a great deal we have left to discuss."

"Such as what, Mr. Harper?" I asked, growing impatient. "I am not the spy you're looking for. Your time would be better spent elsewhere in that regard."

A knock sounded on my door, and I felt a sliver of panic. Harper was right when he said I wouldn't want to be caught with a man in my room. I'd be dismissed, and I wasn't quite ready for that just yet.

"A moment, please," I called.

"Miss Nelson, Miss Burnham is asking for you," Mary's voice came through the door. "Are you well? Do you need some help?"

The doorknob began to turn under my hand. "Thank you, Mary. I'm perfectly fine."

When I glanced over, Harper had a slightly panicked look on his face. Maybe he'd be in as much trouble as I would if he were caught. "I'm sorry I've taken too long. I'll be down to Miss Burnham's room in just a moment."

After a second, the knob returned to its original position, and I could hear footsteps retreating down the corridor. I breathed a sigh of relief. "I think you should leave now, sir. I have work to do."

"Yes, Mr. Burnham will be expecting me. My apologies for disturbing you, Miss Nelson. No doubt our paths will cross again before too long."

I opened the door and stepped aside. "Good day, Mr. Harper."

He glanced both ways down the hallway before he left, and I closed the door behind him. I breathed out and brought my hand to my lips. While I had started out the morning with a clear frame of mind, now I didn't know what to think.

My gaze went to my father's pocket watch, and I bolted to the table to pick it up. How fortunate that Harper hadn't seen it! No doubt he would have been inquisitive, and with the Sinclair name engraved on the cover, I might not have been able to redirect his attention away from me.

Oh, why hadn't I been intelligent enough to leave it behind before coming to this house? I clung to it for sentimental reasons. It wouldn't actually help me discover the truth.

Shaking my head, I slipped the watch's chain around my neck, concealing the time-piece in its usual hiding place before I set off to Eugenia's room.

EUGENIA WAS SITTING in front of the window. She turned in her chair as I entered, having been waiting for me. "Oh there you are," she exclaimed, gesturing for me to come to her side. "I am so happy, Nelson, and it's all thanks to you!"

"Mr. Landon has proposed?" I'd expected Mary to be eager to share that bit of news.

She shook her head. "Well, not exactly, but he asked if he might speak to my father. If Papa gives his blessing, I think he's going to ask me. And it's all because you took the time to help me."

This time I was the one shaking her head. "He would have come around to it eventually. We simply encouraged him to act sooner than he might have liked."

She laughed softly. "Do you think men are aware we are so manipulative?" Eugenia asked, running her finger over the glass. "That we spend so much time making sure we get their attention so hey will propose to us?"

My mind went immediately to Mr. Harper and his suspicions. "I imagine they are a little aware. After all, they have their mothers, and some of them have sisters. They would have to be the dimmest creatures alive to not notice."

"Well, I have met a few men who aren't particularly intelligent." As our eyes met, we both had to bite back our shared amusement. "At times, you remind me of someone I used to know, Nelson. It is the strangest thing."

Given that I wasn't planning on being present for very much longer, I wasn't immediately wary of that statement. "Oh? And who might that be, Miss Burnham?"

"Someone I haven't thought about in a very long time. One of your former employers, Juliet Sinclair. She was older than me, but we used to play together when my family would spend a summer in the country. Her father and my father were business partners, and invested in the same ventures."

Honestly, I was amazed that she hadn't mentioned me—well, Juliet Sinclair—long before this. "I'm flattered." I moved to the dressing table, straightening a pair of gloves that rested there. I was tempted to ask what inspired the comparison but thought better of it in time.

Out of the corner of my eye, I watched as Eugenia frowned. "I don't know what it is though," she finally said, a note of frustration creeping into her voice. "I suppose she always knew just what to do all the time, the way everyone always seems to know better than I do."

"I think you give us too much credit," I said with a slight laugh. "Sometimes, we make the best we can of situations and hope that we made the right choices."

The door flew open. "Eugenia! You'll never guess what just happened," Calliope exclaimed rushing in, followed closely by Daphne. "Papa has been shut in his office with Mr. Harper, and he is furious!"

"Mr. Harper? Why would he be furious?"

"No, Eugenia. Don't be silly. Papa is the one who is angry," Daphne said with obvious exasperation. "I didn't exactly understand what he was saying, because Old Gray Boots caught us listening at the door, but I don't think I've ever heard papa so angry."

Eugenia's expression became puzzled, but I was fighting back a smirk. Was it petty to feel pleased that Mr. Harper was being taken down a peg or two? Probably. However, I wasn't going to allow any hint of remorse to affect my feelings on the matter. He most certainly had it coming to him after his horrible behavior earlier, and his wild accusations about me were far from the mark.

"There you two are," Miss Graham said as she entered the room. "Did I not tell you both to go to the schoolroom?"

"But we want to be with Eugenia." Calliope stamped a stubborn foot against the floorboards. "We hardly get to see her anymore."

"Girls, you have your studies," Eugenia told them. Something outside the window caught her attention, and she didn't seem to hear the protestations that came from both of her sisters. "He's here."

That simple statement made Daphne and Calliope go silent. "Who is here, my dear?" Miss Graham asked.

Eugenia turned to us, a shining smile on her face. "It's Mr. Landon," she said as though it should have been perfectly obvious. "He told me he wanted to speak to father, but I didn't think he would come so soon! Visiting time isn't for hours."

"Well, that is encouraging, isn't it?" Miss Graham commented. "May I offer my felicitations, Eugenia?"

Blushing, Eugenia prettily protested that it was too soon for such congratulations.

"Eugenia, what if Papa refuses, and you have no other prospects for the season?" Daphne asked in a horrified whisper. "Will you be an old maid?"

The governess grabbed Daphne's arm and spun her around towards the door. "What kind of thought is that, Daphne Burnham?" Miss Graham asked sharply. "Must you always try to shatter your sister's confidence like that? I am thoroughly out of patience with you both."

Surprised, I watched as the woman herded the two younger girls out of the room. Her impatience surprised me. On the surface, Daphne's question may have been a bit outlandish, however, I had taken it as sisterly teasing. There was no reason to berate the girl for such actions.

Eugenia's voice dropped to a concerned whisper. "Nelson? Will father disapprove of Landon?"

"I can think of no reason he would," I said. "In fact, I am certain he only wants you to be happy."

"Please stay awhile," she begged, holding out her hand. I let her pull me onto the chair opposite her. "I know Mama is still asleep, so you won't need to go to her. I always feel more confident when you are with me."

Such a declaration warmed my heart, but sentimentality was sure to make me dissolve into tears. I wanted to avoid that. "Now, worrying will do you no good, Miss Burnham," I told her briskly as I turned to the window. "I have no doubt you will soon be called down to have a few private moments with your Mr. Landon."

Her cheeks flushed an even deeper hue. "See? You have a gift for making me feel better about myself."

"Well, I am not always going to be here, so you must get in the habit of doing it yourself," I said primly. She heaved a sigh and nodded. "I am serious, Miss Burnham."

"I wouldn't think otherwise."

Silence formed between us and I wasn't in a hurry to break it. We sat in front of the window for some time, and then the door opened. Mary appeared, wearing an air of barely contained excitement. "Miss Burnham, Mr. Landon is waiting for you in the drawing room."

Squeezing my hands one last time, Eugenia stood up. She took a deep breath and smoothed her gown. "Thank you, Mary," she said as she walked out.

Mary and I exchanged triumphant looks. "Success," Mary whispered. I smiled as I nodded.

Success, indeed.

Chapter Sixteen

There was rejoicing in all levels of the house when Miss Eugenia Burnham accepted Mr. Gerard Landon's proposal of marriage. The servants were all fond of Eugenia and had been hoping to see her happily settled. Mrs. Burnham was ready to have one daughter off her hands, and Mr. Burnham just wanted his oldest daughter to be happy and secure.

The engagement was even alluded to in the Times no more than three days later, and a celebratory dinner was planned for that night. I worked my fingers to the bone trying to change Eugenia's wardrobe ahead of her need for the gowns. It felt as though I hardly had a moment even to think!

But one evening, after the Burnhams left for a dinner party, I sat at my dressing table, setting aside my hairbrush and meager accessories. I drew a sheet of paper from its case and dipped my quill into a bottle of ink. Maybe once I could see the details of this mystery in writing, it would become clearer in my mind. For a moment, as I stared at the blank paper, I paused to consider just what to put down.

I knew I should be making preparations to leave. After all, there was a dangerous traitor still there. Whoever it was had left the knife in my pillow as a warning. If anyone else were to ask questions, such as Mr. Harper, what would the traitor do? Would it be assumed I was working with Mr. Harper?

"The man could be the death of me," I said with a sigh.

My thoughts went to how I hadn't seen the young man in the house since our confrontation. I wondered what he was doing, and if he was any closer to discovering what he wanted to know. Or was he also at a standstill?

Shaking my head, I turned my attention to the blank sheet in front of me. I scribbled a list of the prominent individuals in the house and added Mr. Harper's name, just for the sake of being thorough. I also made a few brief notes, describing what he'd told me. "He would be playing a dangerous game if he were the traitor," I decided as I looked over it. I drew a line through his name. For now, he was not a suspect.

At the top of the list was Mr. Burnham, and I noted the information he'd revealed during our conversation. He had been my father's friend, and I wanted to think the best of him. However, he knew what Jonathan had been doing, and so he could have betrayed my brother. But, he hadn't been here when the pointed warning was left in my pillow in the form of the paperknife. Unless he'd arranged for a third-party to leave the note, such as his valet, but to what end?

I scratched out his name, tentatively freeing him from suspicion. It took longer for me to do so for Mrs. Burnham, but I eventually decided that she was too self-absorbed to concern herself with politics. Eugenia, Calliope, and Daphne were innocent of any wrongdoing unless the younger pair's mischievous, immature behavior could be considered a crime, and I removed them from the list.

Faced with the list of servants, I paused. Anyone of them could have left the knife in my pillow. Which reminded me I ought to learn what Wilder had discovered in that regard. I capped my ink, folded my list, and stood up. After hiding the papers in my pocket, I headed for the door in search of the one person who could give me the insight I needed.

Evenings always brought a calm to the lower levels of the house. I rapped my knuckles against the door of Wilder's office. It took several moments before the butler called out a sharp, "Yes? Who is it?"

"It's Miss Nelson, sir." I laid my hand on the doorknob in anticipation of his summons. "Might I have a few words with you?"

Nearly a minute of silence passed, and I began to wonder if he had heard me. The doorknob turned, and I pulled my hand away. A very flustered, blushing Mrs. Wilder opened the door. "Please come in, Miss Nelson." Her hair was mussed, and she smoothed her gown. "Wilder and I were going over...the accounts."

Oh. My cheeks burned with embarrassment as I realized I had intruded upon a private moment between the married couple. "Of course," I managed to say. I found I couldn't look her in the eye. "I'm sorry to have interrupted you. When would be a better time for me to return? Perhaps tomorrow?"

Wilder appeared behind the housekeeper. "What is it, Miss Nelson?" he asked impatiently, straightening his jacket.

"I was curious whether you have made any discovery concerning the paper knife," I said, eager to move past this awkward situation.

The pair exchanged looks, and they both moved back. "Please come in and have a seat." I accepted the seat across from his desk. Mrs. Wilder stood behind her husband when he sat down. "I informed Mr. Burnham of what occurred, and he is very concerned. It seems there have been far too many instances of a someone being here that should not."

Mr. Burnham was still angry about Mr. Harper's coming and goings, but I knew that the young man hadn't been the one to leave the knife. "Mr. Burnham did not recognize the knife?"

"He did not."

It would have been too easy if he had, and I considered carefully what to say next. Asking if one of the staff could be a traitor seemed too blunt. "May I have the knife back?"

Both Wilders looked startled. "Why would you want it returned?" Mrs. Wilder asked.

"Oddly enough, it looks familiar to me, though, for the life of me, I cannot recall where I have seen it," I explained. "I was hoping if I could take it to study, it might jog my memory."

Wilder pulled a drawer open, drawing the knife out. "Mr. Burnham may want it," he warned as he held it out to me.

"And I will return it immediately if he should." I glanced over the design on the handle for a moment before I slipped it into my pocket. "Mr. Wilder, Mrs. Wilder, I have no wish to offend you, but I do have another question. Is there anyone on staff that you feel could be involved in questionable activities?"

If I thought my request to have the paper knife back had startled them, this question completely stunned them. "Of course not!" Mrs. Wilder exclaimed, her tone bristling defensively. "How dare you think we would hire a criminal!"

"I don't believe that at all!" How to explain without giving too much away? "It's just that...it is possible that someone may feel they have no other choice in a situation."

Wilder frowned at me. "Miss Nelson, do you believe you are in danger? Have you been threatened before?"

"No, I have not. But it was brought to my attention that nothing is quite how it should be here."

"What do you mean by that?" Mrs. Wilder demanded, still defensive.

Her tone spurred me to respond in a sharper tone than I intended. "I mean exactly what I say! Is it normal, do you suppose, for a lady's maid to be threatened with a knife plunged into her pillow? For young gentlemen to come in and out at any hour of the day?"

The butler held up his hand, cutting off his wife. "Mr. Burnham has expressed concerns," he admitted. I could only imagine that he was sharing this information because I was already a part of the events. "I would personally vouch for any of our staff, Miss Nelson. They are hardworking and honest individuals."

"That is all I need to know."

"Though Miss Graham," he began to say, before stopping himself.

"What about Miss Graham?" I asked, reminded that I'd never had the opportunity to ask about the errands that took her from the house so often. How had I forgotten about that?

"She did mention that Bridges has had some family crisis," Mrs. Wilder reluctantly said. "I did think it strange that the valet would choose to confide in a governess."

Perhaps the pair had been more circumspect in their feelings for each other around the servants. Humming a note, I stood up. "Thank you. I appreciate you taking time away from your...accounts."

Before they could react to that impertinent parting statement, I hurried out and returned to my room. I sat back down at the dressing table. While the Wilders could certainly be mistaken in the servants under them, they did know them better than I. It took only a few seconds to draw lines through most of the names left on my list, leaving me with only two: Bridges and Miss Graham.

"Miss Graham, what are you involved with?" I said aloud as I contemplated her name.

She had become close to Bridges, but why would my old governess threaten me? Had someone convinced her to do so? If so, was that person Bridges?

The way he was able to appear out of nowhere and watch everything was uncanny. And hadn't he reacted strangely to me when I had arrived?

I circled his name and folded the page, wondering whether there was some place safe I could keep my list. Someone —Bridges?—had already entered my room once. Until I could prove the valet guilty or innocent, I had to make sure he didn't know I suspected him.

And though I wanted to keep it where I could consult again, I consigned it to the fire.

Once the paper had disintegrated in the flames, I needed to hear Miss Graham's point of view. I left my room for the second time and made my way to the nursery where Calliope and Daphne still slept. I found the two girls there, arguing over a game, but there was no sign of the governess.

"Gray Boots? She said she had to go out," Calliope explained when I asked. She shrugged her shoulders. "She does that a lot."

"At this late hour?" I glanced at the windows that looked out to the darkness.

"We're used to it by now. Are you going to stay and play with us? Callie is cheating and won't stop."

"You both are old enough to amuse yourselves," I said firmly, having no desire to be drawn into their squabbling. Ignoring their protests, I left the room and firmly closed the door. They weren't that intent on having my company because they didn't follow me as I walked down to the library.

"Oh, Miss Graham," I murmured as I warmed my hands at the fire. The more I thought about it, the more I suspected that my former governess was involved in something dangerous. She and I had never been close, as sometimes is the case between governesses and their charges, but I had no desire for her to be embroiled in any suspicious activities.

Making sure the door was open, I settled into a chair to wait for her return. If there was one habit I remember from when she taught me, she always perused bookshelves for something new to read each night, whether she had finished a volume or not. This would be where she would come once she returned from wherever she had gone.

SEVERAL HOURS PASSED and I was on the verge of searching her out when the governess came in. Curled up in a chair, I straightened as she walked directly to the bookshelf. "Miss Graham," I said, closing the volume I had vainly been trying to read while I waited. I rose from the chair to face her.

She gave a sharp gasp and spun around. "Juliet, what are you doing in here?"

"Waiting for you. Where did you go?"

"Not that it's any of your business, but I was delivering a note for Mr. Bridges." Miss Graham smoothed her skirt, looking flustered despite her confidence. "You shouldn't be here, Juliet."

"Here as in the library, or here as in this house?"

She glared at me. "Both."

I held my hands up in a placating way. "I will not argue with you, Miss Graham. I am more than ready to leave this house, but I can't do that until the traitor has been uncovered. So I need you to be honest with me. Why does Bridges need you to deliver messages for him?"

"Is this an interrogation?"

"It's a simple question."

For a moment, I was afraid she wasn't going to answer. "Again, it's none of your business," the governess told me. "His sister is extremely ill, and he's been concerned about her. Obviously, with all his duties now that Mr. Burnham has returned, he cannot leave to see to her. So, he writes to her instead to encourage her to get well."

"And no one else, none of the footmen, could deliver the message?" I asked skeptically. "I find that hard to believe."

"It doesn't matter what you believe," Miss Graham said sharply.

Her behavior was unreasonable, more so than I had expected. "You're right. It doesn't."

Somehow, I had to convince her that there was a real problem, and Bridges was connected to it. "But how about what Mr. Burnham believes? A traitor has been traced to this house, and has already threatened me once."

Startled, Miss Graham stared at me. "A traitor? Threatened you? Threatened you how? You're not making any sense. What are you talking about, Juliet?"

I pulled the knife from my pocket. "This was left in my room some time ago," I told her, choosing not to go into the details. Her face paled. "Do you recognize it?"

"Don't you?"

"If I did, I would not be asking you. How do you know this blade?"

"Juliet, it belonged to your brother. He purchased it before he left your father's house the last time. He was very proud of it."

The blade shook in my hand. "What?" I looked down at the blade. The memory of my brother trimming the pages of a new book for me the day before he left came to mind, and I knew she was right. I had only seen it that one time, I was sure, thus accounting for why I did not immediately recognize it. But why? Who would have stolen my brother's knife and leave it in my pillow that way? "No."

"Bridges wouldn't have it," Miss Graham said, her tone insistent. "You must have brought it with you."

"Why would I have my brother's knife, and why would I bring it with me? It is you who is not making sense now."

"Your insistence on believing that Bridges is a traitor doesn't make sense either."

"Why are you so defensive?" I asked, surprised by her insistence on the matter. "You know there's some truth to what I'm saying, don't you?"

She scoffed. "You're ridiculous." A thoughtful expression came to her face. "I'm beginning to think that the loss of your family affected your mind, Juliet. You are not yourself. Let me help you. You must return to your aunt and everything will be fine."

"Are you trying to imply that I am insane?" I asked, taking a step back. She'd called me foolish and reckless, but never insane. She couldn't mean it! "Are you so desperate to get me out of this house, Miss Graham?"

"A proper lady wouldn't have attempted this masquerade you have put yourself through," Miss Graham responded, her tone becoming gentle. "I can't be the only one who has seen this. Perhaps this is the reason, Mr. Bladen—"

"Don't you dare bring his name into this!" This was not going as I had expected, and I had to bring it to an end. "I'd hoped that you would help me. I see that it was wrong of me to assume that your loyalty to your country would persuade you."

There was a pause as we stared at each other. "I'm going to tell Mr. Burnham what you have done," the governess said. "The lies must stop. You need help, Juliet."

My eyes widened. "You gave me your word that you wouldn't!"

"You've taken this pretense too far," Miss Graham said, a note of smugness saturating her voice. "If you don't leave before tomorrow morning, I will reveal your secret. You will be ruined, Juliet. Any hope you have of achieving a good marriage will be gone."

That threat made me straighten my spine. So, this was the way she wanted to play things? "My entire family was murdered, and you think all I have to be concerned about is whether or not I will find a husband? But very well. I accept your ultimatum. I will pack my things and leave at dawn."

Kneeling down, I picked up the paper knife. Knowing it had been my brother's made it important to me now. "Good evening, Miss Graham," I said before walking out of the room. I felt more shaken than when Mr. Harper had attacked me or even when I'd found the knife.

Miss Graham had questioned my sanity. No doubt many in society would agree with her. The thought of being sent to the Bethlehem Asylum terrified me. Though I knew only my uncle, Frederick Faircroft, could have me sent to that place, I had no reason to believe that he would accept any story I had to tell him in explanation of my actions.

I had to get out.

Chapter Seventeen

Once I was safely in my room, with the chair wedged under the doorknob, I pulled my carpet-bag out from under my bed, where I had made sure to keep it close. It didn't take long for me to deposit my few belongings into it, and I set it by the door. All I would have to do was grab it on my way out.

But I wasn't about to leave without making sure some kind of warning reached Mr. Burnham. I sat at the dressing table and applied my quill to paper. The first letter was more of a note. I used wax to seal it and set it aside. Pulling a fresh sheet of paper, I began to outline everything I had seen; every suspicious behavior I had seen from Bridges since I had arrived.

It wasn't much, to be sure, but perhaps it would be enough.

This one I addressed to Mr. Burnham before I sealed it as well. I couldn't trust that it would reach his hands if I left it on his desk, though. So, I slipped it into my pocket to have it delivered to him once I was out of the house. The last few notes were ones of farewell, and these I propped against the mirror where they were sure to be found once I was discovered missing.

My task completed, I checked my watch. It was nearing the time for the Burnhams to return but I had enough time to send the most important of my communications. I picked up the sealed note I had written first and went to the door, where I pulled the chair free of the knob. Opening the door, I glanced out into the hallway. It was all quiet, and I slipped out.

Feeling nervous and shaky, I returned to the lower levels once more, this time to the kitchen. As I expected, the footmen were alone at the table, drinking. They both jerked to their feet when I entered. "Miss Nelson," Edward, the flirtatious one of the pair, flashed a grin at me. "What brings you to us?"

"I would like to have this sent round to Mr. Harper's residence," I informed him, not caring what they would naturally assume by that. My reputation in this household no longer mattered. I held the missive out to him. "It is vitally important that this is delivered tonight."

Raising his eyebrow, Edward took it from me and made a show of studying it. "Mr. Harper, hmm? I didn't know you'd set your cap at him, Miss Nelson. You aim high. What do I get out of this?"

I flicked a pointed glance toward the decanter on the table. "I will not tell Mr. Burnham that you have a habit of drinking his good brandy." Better that than offering up the few coins I had brought along to bribe him. I didn't know whether I would need them or not.

The other footman scowled. "You've convinced me," Edward said immediately. "I will leave immediately, Miss Nelson."

Waiting until I saw him go out the door, I took the time to take a deep breath. "You look pale, Miss Nelson," the other footman said, leaning forward. "Is anything wrong?"

I walked out of the kitchen without giving him an answer. Now I had one last letter to put into place. I chose to go to the main staircase, instead of the back one. As I neared the top, I caught sight of Miss Graham and Bridges talking together in front of Mr. Burnham's bedroom door.

My steps froze as the valet turned towards me. He offered me a slight bow, a smile playing on his lips. I inclined my head in acknowledgment, determined not to show my fear. "I imagine the Burnhams will be returning soon," I called out, going up the last few steps. I walked towards them boldly. They couldn't hurt me here where anyone could come along.

"I bow to your expert opinion, Miss Nelson," Bridges said, with that ever-present mocking note. "Miss Graham tells me that you will be leaving us soon."

Miss Graham was watching me with a narrow-eyed expression. "Where have you been?"

"Sending a note to a friend." They both exchanged quick glances as I continued, "As I will be without employment tomorrow, I decided I needed to make sure I have a place to go. You understand that it would be impolite to show up on their doorstep without a word of warning."

Bridges took a step in my direction but was stopped from coming any closer by the sound of the front door opening.

"Just because you are engaged to Mr. Landon does not mean you can blatantly ignore a viscount's conversation, Eugenia!" Mrs. Burnham's voice could be heard a moment later.

"I am not a flirt, Mama," Eugenia said in answer. "How would Mr. Landon have felt if I had responded to such outrageous comments in front of him?"

"It appears we both must return to our duties now," I remarked, meeting Bridges' gaze. "Good night, Miss Graham. I do hope Daphne and Calliope did not get up to too much mischief while you were out."

I stepped around them and hurried to Mrs. Burnham's dressing room. Mary was pouring hot water into the pitcher for me, and her presence kept me from leaning against the door to catch my breath. "I can put Miss Eugenia to bed," she said. "You're looking very tired tonight, Miss Nelson."

No wonder, considering everything I had been through in the short span of a few hours. "Do not worry, Mary," I told her, forcing a slight smile. I wanted to say some kind of farewell before I left. "I don't mind. I know you have more duties than I do."

"No, I insist."

Arguing would only make her suspicious, so I reluctantly gave in and hoped the letter I had left for Eugenia would be enough. "Thank you, Mary."

Mary frowned. "Miss Nelson, is something wrong?"

"I can't explain everything right now." How I wished that I could. Hopefully, the bare details would be enough to satisfy her and keep her from danger. "Avoid Bridges if you can. He is not who he pretends to be. Please, trust me, Mary."

"Are you in trouble, Miss Nelson?"

The door swung open, ending our conversation. "I do not understand my daughter," Mrs. Burnham complained as she flounced in. She tossed her shawl at me, and I was quick to keep it from hitting the floor. Mary bobbed a quick curtsey and made her exit. "The viscount was merely polite and what does Eugenia do? She focuses only on Mr. Landon! What am I to do with her?"

I kept quiet as I readied her for her bed. As she recited her list of the grievances she had suffered that evening, I didn't listen to a word of them. Once my work was complete, I closed the door, feeling a sense of relief that I would not have to face her as a lady's maid ever again.

Breathing a sigh of relief that the hallway was empty, I rushed up to my room. I made sure to wedge the chair back against the door and made my final preparations. I couldn't be sure how long Bridges would be occupied with seeing to Mr. Burnham, and I needed to escape before he came to silence me for good.

Any man who would leave a knife in a pillow would not shrink back from using violence to keep me from revealing his treachery.

Could I take the chance that Miss Graham had kept her promise? I had never known her to go back on her word before, but had her emotions blinded her to Bridges' actions? She could have told him all, thinking she was helping me back on the course she thought I needed to be on. Did he know, even now, that I was not Julie Nelson but Juliet Sinclair?

I decided I had to take the chance, making sure the paper knife was still in my pocket. If circumstances went from bad to worse, maybe it would save my life. It would be as though my brother were protecting me once again.

Breathing out, I tried to steady my nerves. My pelisse felt constricting as I tied my bonnet ribbons under my chin. I placed the notes where they would be visible to anyone entering the room and blew out my candle. Picking up my carpet bag, I pulled the chair free and opened the door. Cautiously, I checked both ways, making sure no one was in sight before I slipped out.

I tried to keep my footsteps as quiet as possible. The floor creaked under my feet as it always did when I walked, only the sound seemed louder than ever before. No one appeared to question or stop me.

A creak behind me made me pause, my breath catching in my throat. I looked over my shoulder, but there was no one there. After waiting a moment with no one showing themselves, I hurried to the door.

Turning the lock only took a moment and then I was out of the house. I sent a quick glance both ways down the street and could see no sign of a hansom cab. Stifling a sigh, I set off down the pavement, eager to make the walk as quickly as possible.

Again, I heard a sound behind me, only this time I knew for sure it was footsteps. I started to turn, but an arm came around my neck. "Leaving at this time of night, Miss Nelson?" Bridges asked, seeming not to notice as I struggled. He didn't even flinch when I jammed my elbow into his side. "That seems rather suspicious, don't you think? What will the master think when he learns of this in the morning?"

"Why do we not tell him of it now?" I challenged before his arm tightened and cut my voice off. I could have said several impolite words a lady shouldn't even know right then. Why had I not screamed when I had the chance?

"I think we should take this conversation somewhere more private, Miss Nelson," Bridges said in my ear. He firmly dragged me in the opposite direction I wanted to go. Of course, I wasn't about to make it easy on him and dug my heels into the floor as much as I could. He solved this by lifting me off my feet and carrying me.

Feeling light-headed, I kicked my feet as he manhandled me further away from the Burnham residence. "What happened to Marie?" Bridges asked in my ear. Who was Marie?

Unable to speak, I shook my head as much as I was able. "You took her place, Miss Nelson. Surely you know what happened to keep her from my side. What gave her away?"

Was he referring to the original Miss Nelson who had missed her interview? My mind raced with that information. Had she been working with Bridges?

Bridges' arm loosened slightly, and I was able to take a quick breath. "I don't know," I managed to say. I honestly knew nothing about the woman. It had been entirely coincidental that I arrived at the very time she had missed her interview and had been mistaken for her. Mrs. Burnham had certainly not noticed the discrepancy between Marie Nelson's letters of recommendations and the Julie Nelson who had begun working for her. Don't even know how Mrs. Burnham had those letters in the first place. "I swear I have never heard of her."

He spun me around and grabbed my shoulders. I bit back a cry of pain as my shoulder protested the rough treatment. Bridges shook me roughly. "Did they not think I would suspect a strange woman using Marie's name?" He gave a slight laugh. "That the added 'Julie' would disguise you?"

"Who are they?" I asked in bewilderment as I cast my gaze to the nearest house. A few of the windows had a soft glow as though candles were burning in the upper windows. If I screamed now, would anyone hear me? Deciding there was nothing to keep me from trying, I opened my mouth to do so. This time I was cut off by his open hand connecting with my left cheek. The force turned my head as pain stung my cheek.

"You are in a very precarious situation, Miss Nelson," Bridges said with a sneer. "Don't endanger yourself any more than you have already foolishly done."

Straightening my head, I glared at him as my hand stole into my pocket. My brother's knife was still there. "Miss Graham should have warned you that I will do as I wish, no matter what anyone says." I pulled the knife out and stabbed at him. He cried out as the blade dug into his arm.

He let go of me, and I let out the shrillest scream I had ever managed in my life. That earned me another blow to that immediately made my ears ring. He grabbed my wrist and twisted, forcing me to drop the weapon.

Before I could recover, Bridges locked his hands around my throat. "I have a good thing going here, and you nearly destroyed that. Information has a high price in France. I almost have enough to for me to abandon this tedious life of servitude. I will set myself up as a proper gentleman.

At any other time, I would have found it interesting that he had kept from killing me to ask about Marie Nelson. Instead, I clawed at his wrists while he slowly tightened his grip. My kicks had no effect, and I was unable to keep up the attack for more than a few seconds.

Black spots began dancing in front of my eyes. I regretted that I hadn't sent a note in recent days to Aunt Beth. How would she feel when she learned of my death? My escapades had already worried her so much. Did she know how much I adored her? Tears sprung to my eyes. I didn't want to die. Not like this. Not so soon.

Who would clear my family's name? Who would find the man that murdered my brother and created the 'accident' that took my parents?

"It's no use struggling any longer," Bridges whispered. "It's all over now."

Chapter Eighteen

Darkness filled my vision, and the rushing sound of my racing pulse was loud in my ears. But I thought I heard something beyond that: the sound of a voice shouting my name. "Miss Nelson. Miss Nelson!"

Who was it? The voice was male, I could hear that much, but it seemed to be coming from such a long distance. Was it Mr. Harper? Had he come?

A second before I was certain I was about to lose consciousness completely, Bridges' hands were suddenly gone from my neck and I felt the cool night air against my skin. I fell, trying to cough and suck in blessed air at the same time. As my hearing and vision cleared, the sound of a fist meeting flesh rang out, and Bridges hit the ground a few feet away from me.

Then, someone was crouching down in front of me. "Miss Nelson, are you hurt?" Mr. Harper asked, grasping my shoulders. There was concern written on his face.

If I hadn't been sure of his innocence before, now I knew for certain. "I'll live," I managed to say before coughing again. My throat hurt like nothing I'd ever experienced before and my head ached. Without a doubt, I was going to be sore in the morning.

Putting my hand in his, I accepted his help in rising. It was then that I realized we were not alone. Two men I didn't recognize were hauling Bridges up. Wilder held a lantern, looking concerned and disheveled. Mr. Burnham was also there, speaking to an unfamiliar gentleman.

"Let's get you inside," Mr. Harper said to me. "I think you could use a strong drink."

If I hadn't felt so miserable, I would have laughed at that. He wrapped his arm around me, supporting me in a rather comforting way. I only went a few steps before I stopped. "I have to ask him," I said, trying to turn. Mr. Harper wouldn't let me though. "I have to ask Bridges about the Sinclairs."

"Someone will question him, I promise," Mr. Harper assured me. "Right now, you need to recover. You've had a great shock."

A great shock? That had to be the understatement of the night. Mary and Mrs. Wilder were at the door when we reached it. "Oh, Miss Nelson, what has happened?" the housekeeper exclaimed. She reached out her hands. "We'll see to her from here, Mr. Harper."

Was it my imagination or did Mr. Harper seem reluctant to release me? He did, though, and I went from his support to Mrs. Wilder's. "Mr. Burnham and I will have questions for Miss Nelson," Mr. Harper said. He gave a formal bow, an action that seemed ridiculous in the circumstances, and then turned to hurry away.

I would have to thank him later for saving my life.

"What happened to you?" Mrs. Wilder demanded as she guided me inside. She was wearing a dressing gown over her nightgown, showing she'd been pulled from her bed. "We heard a scream and then Mr. Harper was pounding at the door."

"I'm sorry to have disturbed you all," I apologized insincerely. My voice was hoarse, it hurt to talk, and all I wanted was to be in my bed.

"Edward, do something useful and fetch Miss Nelson some brandy," Mrs. Wilder snapped. I lifted my eyes to find that the majority of the household staff seemed to have assembled downstairs. "The rest of you return to your beds! You all have duties to see to come dawn."

That sent the majority of the gawkers running. Mrs. Wilder firmly steered me to her room and sat me at the table. Edward appeared in the doorway with the decanter I had seen at his side earlier. The housekeeper snatched it from him, along with the glass, and then shooed him away.

"Drink this, if you can," Mrs. Wilder urged, pouring a small amount of brandy and pressing the glass into my hand. "I wonder if we ought to summon a physician."

I wanted to protest that all I needed was some sleep, but decided that the pain of speaking made it not worth the effort. I sipped the strong liquid, flinching at the pain in my throat. A warm feeling slowly spread, and the trembling in my hands that I hadn't even noticed began to still.

"I have Miss Nelson's bag," Mary announced, coming into the room. She looked curious. "Bridges has been taken away."

"I always knew that man was trouble," Mrs. Wilder muttered. "Attacking defenseless young women in the night? Horrible! I hope hangs for this!"

She didn't need to know the truth, and I just nodded in agreement. Bridges certainly deserved to be punished for what he'd done: selling information to France and attacking me, though I'm sure an attack on a maid wouldn't rank very high in the eyes of the government. If only I could know he'd been the one to kill my family, I would be satisfied.

My head was pounding, and I forced myself to my feet. "I would like my bed now, please."

"Of course," Mrs. Wilder said in the most motherly tone I'd ever heard from her. "Mary, help her along. Make sure no one annoys her. In fact, I think it might be best if you were to stay with her tonight."

Mary had her hands full as she tried to carry my bag, hold up a candle, and put an arm around me. I almost smiled at the comicalness of it. I took my carpet bag from her. She breathed a sigh of relief and lent me her support.

The hardest part was facing the stairs. By the time I reached the top, I felt unusually short of breath.

"Do you need to rest?" Mary asked with concern.

Shaking my head, I continued. Reaching my tiny room, I sank onto my bed while Mary bustled around. She left the candle on the dressing table, pulled my things from my bag, and then helped me into my nightgown. She didn't say anything about the pocket watch that I had hung around my neck, merely set it aside where I could see it.

It was a relief to pull the blankets up to my chin. Mary pulled a chair close to the side of my bed. "You don't have to stay," I told her, knowing just how uncomfortable that chair was if you sat on it for longer than five minutes.

"I'll stay until you are asleep," Mary responded firmly. "And don't you worry about your duties tomorrow. I'll handle them."

Too tired to argue, I closed my eyes. Tomorrow would come too quickly for me and with it repercussions from the night.

WITH A SHARP GASP, I opened my eyes. The nightmare that had startled me awake faded almost instantly and left me feeling breathless as I stared up at the ceiling. Light filled the room and did nothing to ease the headache that still pounded behind my eyes.

Groaning, I closed my eyes and thought about what had happened. "Aunt Beth is going to be furious," I murmured, grimacing at the hoarseness that still plagued my voice.

Never one to lie abed, I forced myself to sit up and then to rise to my feet. I had to move slowly to dress, missing the help Mary normally would have given me, but a glance at my watch showed that it was near one in the afternoon. The maid was no doubt busy with duties, both hers and mine.

Had the notes I'd written been found yet? Or were they still waiting to be picked up? What would everyone say when they read my words?

I made myself face the mirror. My gown did nothing to hide the bruises that now decorated my neck. There was also a bruise on my cheek where Bridges had struck me. Dark circles shadowed my eyes.

In short, I looked a complete wreck.

The door opened, and I spun around. "Oh, you're up," Mary said with satisfaction. There was a tray of tea in her hands which she laid on the table. "I was hoping you would be. Mr. Burnham has asked after you and Mr. Harper has arrived. They will want to speak to you."

"Thank you," I whispered.

Her eyes took in the reminders of Bridges' attack, and she paled. "Oh, you must be in dreadful pain."

"I will survive," I quickly assured her. How far we had come since I first stepped foot in the house when she had detested me on sight!

Mary straightened herself and nodded. "Of course," she said. "I will leave you to your tea. I will let you know when Mr. Burnham requires you."

Nodding my thanks, I poured myself some tea, and she left the room. The very idea of even attempting to eat made my throat ache and I couldn't eat a bite of the toast. I sipped at the tea, forcing each swallow of liquid down my throat.

I wondered if Eugenia had handed my letter to her father. It would go a long way to explain everything that had happened. I certainly did not want to endure lengthy questioning with my throat so sore! I'd only put the bare minimum of details in my note to Mr. Harper, which had been enough to bring him running in the night.

As I remembered how Mr. Harper had come to my rescue, my heart danced to an irregular rhythm. Without him, I would be dead, and that wasn't something I was about to forget any time soon.

Could I admit everything now? Should I finally confide my story to someone who would understand?

A light tap on the door tore me from my musings, and I looked up as Mrs. Wilder entered. "The master is asking for you if you feel up to speaking with him." She scanned my appearance, failing to conceal a scowl. "He is in the library with Mr. Harper."

I set aside my teacup, which still contained half of the tea I'd poured for myself. Hardly enough sustenance for anyone, but I couldn't bring myself to force it down. "I will need a moment to fix my hair."

Mrs. Wilder strode forward. "Hold still." She picked up my hairbrush, which Mary must have pulled out while I slept. Her reflection smiled at mine. "Did you not know I was once the personal maid of Mr. Burnham's mother?"

The notion had never occurred to me. I remained still as Mrs. Wilder expertly arranged my hair into a rather attractive knot. She tutted as she examined the bruises on my neck. "Keep your shawl close around your neck," she advised. "It will do no one any good to ask questions that are better left unspoken."

I nodded and pulled my carpet bag closer to retrieve my shawl. When I looked up, the housekeeper was watching me. "I suppose we will be seeking a new lady's maid now," she said with a shake of her head, "and just when we were getting used to you and your ways."

All I could do was offer a wry smile in answer. I slung my shawl around, pulling it around my neck, being careful not to aggravate the bruises. Mrs. Wilder stayed behind me as I made my way down the stairs. She remained in the doorway, watching me like a hawk as I approached the library door.

Like a good servant, I opened the door and stepped in. Mr. Burnham and Mr. Harper were seated in front of the fireplace. "You asked to see me, sir?" I said as they both looked in my direction.

"Miss Nelson!" Mr. Harper exclaimed, scrambling to his feet. He pulled a chair close to where he and Mr. Burnham were. "How are you feeling today? Have you recovered?" He paused. "That was a stupid question. Forgive me. Of course, you have not."

It amused me that he was so flustered. A far cry from the suspicious man who had invaded my room to demand answers! I sank into the seat he'd put in place for me and turned my attention to Mr. Burnham, who hadn't risen.

"You caused quite a stir last night, Miss Nelson," he remarked as Mr. Harper sat across from me. "Did Mrs. Wilder send for the doctor?"

I shook my head. "It was not necessary." I tried to clear my throat of the hoarseness that persisted but that only caused more pain.

Mr. Burnham raised an eyebrow at me. "If you insist." He held up the letter I'd sent him through Eugenia. "I must say you built an interesting theory about Bridges. It was foolish of you to approach Miss Graham knowing she had an attachment to my valet. You must have suspected she would betray you."

I'd been relying on her loyalty to a former student, but I couldn't very well explain that to him, could I? I lifted a shoulder in a shrug. "I wanted to give him the benefit of the doubt," I responded evasively. "He was selling information?"

My employer nodded once. "He has, so far, resisted revealing his contact, but I have every confidence we will extract it from him in time."

I dropped my gaze. I didn't want to know that Bridges was probably being tortured. "Did he kill the Sinclairs?"

There was a pause, and I looked up. Mr. Burnham and Mr. Harper were looking at each other. "He has denied any knowledge of Jonathan Sinclair's murder," the older man informed me, a gentle note entering his voice. "And I can safely say that it is unlikely that he was personally responsible as he was with me in London during that time. And I can think of no reason he would cause the accident that took the rest of the Sinclairs."

Something of my emotions must have crossed my face. "Miss Nelson, are you well?" Mr. Harper asked in concern. "Are you in pain?"

"I'm fine," I lied. The physical pain was nothing compared to the hurt in my heart. How I had hoped that this would be the end of my masquerade. Sighing, I opened my eyes. "Thank you for telling me."

Nodding, Mr. Burnham hesitated. "Your letter said you were leaving. I presume this is still the case."

Mr. Harper sent an appalled look at the older man, but I nodded. "Yes, I will gather my things and leave immediately. Will I have a letter of recommendation?"

"I will write it personally. Wilder will have it for you when you leave."

"But where will she go? Where will you go, Miss Nelson?" Mr. Harper asked, turning to me. "You need to rest after last night."

I pushed myself to my feet. "I have an aunt," I responded vaguely. I bobbed my last respectful curtsy and turned on my heel. I think Mr. Harper started to follow me, but a sharp word from Mr. Burnham kept him from doing so. I glanced over my shoulder before I went out the door and Mr. Harper inclined his head towards me.

A smile curved my lips, and I firmly closed the door. I heaved a sigh and walked down the hallway. It was fortunate that my things were already packed. I reached the back staircase and started up.

"You."

Chapter Nineteen

Taking a deep breath, I faced Miss Graham. Her face was blotchy and under her eyes were puffy. However, her hands were clenched tightly and her chin was jutted forward. "This is your doing," she said, her voice a hiss. "Mr. Bridges has been carted away like a common criminal!"

"He tried to kill me!" I protested. I let the shawl I held around my neck fall away, revealing the bruises.

Her eyes went to the bruises, and her face paled even more. "You provoked him," she whispered, almost desperately. "You invented those lies."

"For what reason?" I looked down at her. All I felt at that moment was pity. "Do you think I came into this house with the express purpose to create a lie about Mr. Burnham's valet?"

She glared at me. "I am being turned off, Juliet, without a reference. What am I supposed to do? This was going to be my last position as a governess. I'm not getting any younger."

Tiredly, I shook my head. How much of her hopes she had pinned on Bridges! What did she expect me to do? "I'm sorry, Miss Graham." I turned and continued on my way. My headache was worse than before, and I wanted to hide in a dark room to sleep for a week. Something that would not be possible here.

I'd always idealized love. My parents had loved each other deeply and had been happy. Yet I had never thought about how destructive love could be. I had been given a glimpse of that when Henry had left without a word, but seeing Miss Graham's devastation and blindness at Bridges using her; that was something else entirely.

I had just closed my bag when the door opened. "You're leaving?" Mary asked, a note of panic in her voice. "Why? I thought now that it's over, you'd be staying on!"

"After what I've been through, I have no inclination to stay," I said with a slight smile. I picked up my bonnet and settled it on my head. "You know everything you need to know about caring for Miss Eugenia. There's nothing more I can do here."

"You did not come just to train me," Mary argued.

"That's right, I didn't," I agreed with a smile. She could not know how close she was to the truth. "It's funny how things turn out, isn't it?"

She stared at me in a bewildered sort of way. "But, where will you go?"

Feeling generous, I opened my reticule and drew out a card. "If you feel you need to contact me, you may send a letter to this address. It will find a way to me, wherever I am."

Reluctantly, the maid glanced at the card. "What will I tell Miss Eugenia? She wanted to speak to you, but her mother wouldn't let her come."

"I have left a note for her." I nodded towards the dressing table. The notes I'd left had not been moved and would be all the explanation I could give. I doubted that Mr. Burnham wanted his daughter to know the details of everything that had happened. "It is better this way, Mary."

Her shoulders sagged as she gave in. "I wish you the best, Miss Nelson."

Impulsively, I reached out and hugged her. "And I you, Mary."

The door creaked as Molly pushed it open further. "Mr. Burnham has ordered his carriage ready to take you anywhere you wish, Miss Nelson." There was nothing but curiosity in her voice. Undoubtedly, she had questions that would never be answered.

"Thank you, Molly," I said, stepping back from Mary. I picked up my carpet bag and turned slowly to give the tiny room one last look. I could honestly say that I would not miss it a bit. I nodded once and started for the door.

Both of the maids trailed behind me as I walked down the stairs. Mr. and Mrs. Wilder was waiting by the door. "Goodbye, Miss Nelson," the housekeeper said, extending her hand for me to shake. "Have a safe journey."

I nodded my thanks and turned to the waiting butler. He extended a folded sheet of paper. "Mr. Burnham thanks you for your fine work," he informed me formally, as though I hadn't heard it from the man personally. "He understands that what occurred was not your fault."

With a nod, I took the letter of reference and slipped it into my reticule. With as confident a smile as I could muster, I turned and walked out of the Burnham house for the last time as a servant. Edward assisted me into the waiting carriage. "Where shall the driver set you down?" he asked.

Tired of the pain that came with speaking, I used the last calling card I'd 'borrowed' from Aunt Beth to show him where I wished to be taken. He closed the carriage door, and a moment later, I was off.

Closing my eyes, I leaned my head back against the cushion. It had been so long since I'd been in such comfort and it lulled me into a doze. I didn't even realize the carriage had stopped until the door was pulled open. "Miss Nelson? We've arrived."

First handing out my bag, I accepted his hand in disembarking. For a moment, I stared at the closest door into the house in confusion. We were at the servants' entrance of Faircroft house, and the realization made me want to laugh. I nodded my thanks to the driver, picked up my bag, and strode forward.

Without ringing the bell and waiting, I opened the door and entered the hall. I took a deep breath, taking in the scent of cook's baking from the kitchen. As I stood there, my aunt's maid, Carter, started down the stairs. Her gasp echoed off the marble floor.

"Hello, Carter," I forced a smile through my tiredness. "Is my aunt in her sitting room?"

Carter rushed forward and took the carpet bag from my hand. "Lord, Miss Juliet! You gave me a fright coming out of nowhere!" she exclaimed, examining me. Her eyes widened in shock, something I would have to accustom myself to as the bruises healed. "What have you done to yourself?"

"Acted in an abominably foolish way, of course." I flinched, putting a hand to my throat. "My aunt?"

"She's in the music room," Carter said, regaining her usual composure. "But don't you go walking in on her and giving her a start. I'll announce you and prepare her. I assume you've returned for good this time?"

She didn't wait for my answer as she spun away. "Carlson!" she called out. "Come take Miss Juliet's bonnet and pelisse. Jenny! Where are you, you silly girl?"

The elderly butler appeared, followed by the young maid. As imperturbable as ever, Carlson took my pelisse and bonnet which Carter pulled from me. Jenny grabbed my bag and hurried off with it. I desperately wanted to follow her to my room for some sleep, but I needed to see Aunt Beth first.

"Will you require tea, Miss Juliet?" Carlson asked as Carter hurried off to warn my aunt.

"Yes, please." Tea would be better than nothing. I kept my steps slow as I walked to the music room. How lovely it would be to be able to play the pianoforte once again. I glanced down at my hands, calloused and rougher than they'd ever been before.

I was halfway up the staircase when I heard Aunt Beth cry out. Fear struck my heart, and I rushed up. I spotted Aunt Beth in the doorway, and she held her arms out to me. "Oh, Juliet, dear lambkin!" she exclaimed. "You've come home."

Tears brimmed in my eyes and I hurried to her embrace. "Oh, Aunt Beth."

AUNT BETH CONSIGNED me to my bed immediately, insisting that she could wait for explanations until I was well. After my long hours at the Burnham's house, the rest and lack of discussion were welcome for the first two days. The pain in my throat and my headache faded, though the bruises turned some interesting colors.

But after that, the inactivity began to wear thin, and I begged to be allowed up. Aunt Beth insisted I was not entirely well, and wouldn't hear of me rising. Instead, Carter was instructed to bring me something to occupy my time.

She obligingly provided me with the Times each morning, and I pored over the notices until I found exactly what I was looking for. I penned a letter and bribed the new maid to have it sent for me.

After five days, I insisted and was finally allowed out of my bed. It was a pleasure to put on a lovely pale blue muslin morning gown. Standing in front of a mirror, I studied my appearance and decided I almost look like my old self.

Was I happy about that? I felt as though I had changed in so many ways during my time at the Burnhams' house.

Shaking my head, I sent the maid off and then made my way down to the drawing room. Aunt Beth was seated in front of the window in her favorite chair, and she had her fancy needlework in her lap. "It's so good to see you up and about, Juliet. Are you feeling better?"

"Much better, thank you, Aunt." I dropped a kiss on her cheek before settling into the chair across from her. "And how are you feeling today?"

"I am always well, silly minnow." She waved her hand dismissively. Being called a 'minnow' made me laugh. "I am pleased you've finally returned to where you belong and furious that it took a brutal attack for it to happen. I demand you tell me how it came about!"

I nodded and leaned forward. In as few words as I could, I detailed how I'd learned of a traitor selling information to the French, how I'd then deduced who it was, and what he had attempted to keep me quiet. Aunt Beth listened quietly but attentively, not saying anything until I ended with how Mr. Burnham had sent me away in his carriage.

"A spy," Aunt Beth said, shaking her head. "How dreadful. I hope the errant ratsbane gets what is coming to him."

"I do not doubt that Mr. Burnham and Mr. Harper are seeing to it."

My aunt became thoughtful. "I feel as though I must thank this Mr. Harper for saving you, but of course, he does not know the real you, so I suppose I will be forgiven for not doing so."

"As he does not know of you, I hardly think he or anyone else will hold it against you," I agreed, biting back a smile.

Aunt Beth turned her gaze back to me. "And did you accomplish what you set out to do?"

"I believe Mr. Burnham will counteract the rumors. How could explain that I had been left with more questions? That I felt as though I was not yet done? "The Sinclair name will be free of all suspicion."

"Excellent," she declared, not knowing my inner misgivings. "Mr. Bladen was here yesterday. He seemed anxious when I told him you were unwell. Of course, we cannot allow him to see your poor neck, but I believe that once you are healed, he will be ready to recommence your courtship."

"You do not even ask if I want him to do so."

Her expression turned to one of shock. "Juliet! How can you say so?"

"I have changed these past five years, and no doubt so has he. I don't know if we would be compatible any longer."

Reaching over, Aunt Beth patted my hand. "You must do as you think right, my dear. Only I do not wish for you to become a spinster as I am." My shock must have shown on my face for she hastened to add, "You will always have a home here, of course."

"Thank you, Auntie." I squeezed her hands, giving a slight laugh as I sat back. "It is criminal that we should be maudlin on a day like this. Shall we speak of something else?"

She hummed a note as she picked up her sewing. "What would you like to discuss?"

"You did some traveling when you were younger, did you not? How did you find Bath?"

Epilogue

I wasn't sure whether to be pleased with the fact that I could add yet another new experience to my life. Wedged between a stout woman and a tall, thin man was not exactly comfortable. "What takes you to Bath?" the portly man across from me asked.

"It's where my new employer resides." And where I would be sure to find the next clue to solving my brother's murder. Bridges' may not have had anything to do with it, but somehow he'd come by my brother's paper knife, and I wanted to know how. Of course, I could say nothing of this to the other passengers.

He nodded in understanding and then promptly closed his eyes. A snore came from him a moment later, and I bit my lip to keep from smiling. "Men," the women next to me muttered. "Never trust them, my dear. They will bring you nothing but trouble."

Glancing over, I gave a nod of acknowledgment. Then she too drifted asleep, her chin coming down to rest on her chest. With the other passengers either sleeping or their attention elsewhere, I took the opportunity to open my reticule and withdrew two letters. I glanced at the first, scanning Henry Bladen's writing for a moment before secreting it back inside. I unfolded the second and reread the words I'd almost committed to memory.

Miss Nelson,

I hope this letter finds you in good health and fully recovered from your ordeal.

I bend the rules of propriety this once to share with you the news that Bridges was found dead in his cell. No one knows who smuggled a knife in and killed him. I can only assume that it was the man to whom he passed the information he stole from Mr. Burnham.

Bridges had his suspicions about you from the moment you stepped into that house. It is highly likely that he told his contact of you.

> *Be careful, Miss Nelson. This man has killed once and may do so again.*

O. Harper

> *P.S. This paper knife was found in the Burnham's garden. I believe you used it to defend yourself. I return it to you in the hopes it may aid you in the future, whether it be to trim a sheet of writing paper or to ward off an attacker once again.*

O.H

Breathing out, I returned the letter to my reticule and felt the cold blade of the page knife. Having it near reassured me. I turned my gaze to the passing scenery, bringing me ever closer to the last place my brother had been alive.

Juliet's story will continue in The Debutante (The Sinclair Society, Book Two)

Continue reading for a sneak peek!

The Debutante

(Book Two of The Sinclair Society Series)

JULIET SINCLAIR KNOWS her brother was murdered—now if only she could understand why.

Proving her family innocent of treason is taking a toll on lady-turned-maid Juliet. Her latest investigation has brought her into the service of the spoiled Miss Dunbar and her salacious older brother, who pursues Juliet despite repeated rebuffs. Complicating matters further is the reappearance of Juliet's former beau who has not yet learned to do without her, and a growing attraction between herself and her brother's witty—and handsome—best friend.

Even with these distractions, Juliet begins to piece together the events surrounding her brother's final days—and his connection to a mysterious figure named only as "H." But Juliet's ruse is under threat of revelation, and her blackmailer is one who will not hesitate to burn her unless she gives him what he wants: every document related to her brother's former role as a spy for His Majesty against the French.

Chapter One

When the Season ends in London, fashionable society seeks amusement elsewhere, and that place is Bath. While some with ill-health— imagined or otherwise— took to the waters, others enjoyed the best society had to offer in the way of theater, dancing, and such diversions. There are even those who spend their whole lives in Bath.

Propping my father's watch on my dressing table, I leaned down to check my appearance in the small mirror. My walking dress was of a jaconet muslin and perhaps was too delicate for a lady's maid to be seen in. However, as it was my half-day, I had dressed to please myself.

"But what if Miss Dunbar requires something, Miss Nelson?"

Restraining myself from a sigh, I sent a glance over my shoulder. The housemaid, Eliza, stood by the door, wringing her hands together. She was no older than fifteen and was, in general, a nervous creature. "You will provide whatever it is that Miss Dunbar wishes," I said, struggling to keep my tone reassuring. "You must have done so before my arrival."

"Yes, but Miss Dunbar hates me. She threw a jar of cream at me one day when I took too long to reach her room." Poor Eliza's eyes were wide, and I wondered how she had lasted as long as she had in the house. Seven months must have been some record for this household.

"Then, you must be sure to keep from being late, Eliza. I have no intention of foregoing my few hours away from my duties," I stated firmly, as I straightened. I picked up my bonnet. "As Miss Dunbar has no engagements, I suspect she will spend her afternoon practicing the pianoforte, and she will not be in need of any assistance."

My words did nothing to alleviate the fear on Eliza's face. However, there was nothing more I could say on the matter. Hardening my heart, I tied on my bonnet and picked up my reticule. "I shall return in time to assist Miss Dunbar in dressing for the evening," I said.

Her cheeks flushing, Eliza scurried out of my room. I plucked my father's watch from the dressing table and placed it safely in my reticule to carry with me. It was one of the few items I made sure to keep close by for fear of someone happening to it.

I left my room, taking care to close the door firmly behind me. Keeping my belongings secure had become highly critical in the past few months.

"Why, Miss Nelson."

The male voice made my skin crawl. "Mr. Dunbar," I responded, lifting my gaze to the face of the oldest Dunbar son.

Daniel Dunbar was a handsome man, and he knew it. He was tall and had the build of a man who frequented Gentleman Jackson's academy. From the moment he first saw me in his father's house, he had been persistent in his attempts to garner my affection.

From what the housekeeper, Mrs. Dobbs, had said to me, the last lady's maid had been dismissed in disgrace from the consequences of falling for the charming man.

Such a fate would not befall me.

"It's your half-day, isn't it?" Mr. Dunbar asked, his blue eyes flicking over my appearance in a way that made me shudder. His smile widened as though he liked what he saw. "Permit me to walk with you." As he spoke, he extended his arm for me to take.

"No, thank you. I am in no mood for company."

His eyes focused on my face, darkening with annoyance. "Miss Nelson, everyone desires company."

"Not everyone," I said, striding forward boldly. He stepped in front of me to block my way down the back staircase. "Sir, kindly permit me to pass by. I have declined your company and can think of no reason for you to be on this level of the house. Good day."

Moving aside, Mr. Dunbar offered a mocking bow as I swept past him. While I hoped that my continued refusal of his attention would bore him, I feared he was fascinated with the idea I might be uninterested and thus worth pursuing. Somehow, I would have to find a way to hurry my investigation so that I could leave as soon as possible.

I had been in Bath two weeks and had learned nothing new of my brother Jonathan's untimely death. In fact, I had not come across anyone who had ever known him. Such was the obstacle of being in a place where people came and went so easily, something that had not occurred to me before my arrival.

However, I could not rest until I had tried every avenue open to me.

AS I WALKED ALONG THE pavement, I passed many people who were taking advantage of the beautiful weather. Young ladies were giggling and gossiping together as they walked. Gentlemen strode along with confidence.

I was careful to keep my head down and avoided all eye contact. The last thing I wanted was for anyone to recognize me as Miss Juliet Sinclair, and with so many people in Bath, the risk was higher than it had ever been in London.

Fortunately for me, my destination was not a well-traveled place. Once I left the confines of the streets of Bath, I was reminded of the walks I used to take when I was at home in the country with my parents. Birds sang in the trees around me, and the sun shone down, warming my face.

It had taken me the entirety of my last half- day to locate the right parish register that contained where my brother Jonathan was buried. By that point, it had been too late on my previous half- day for me to visit his grave. Now, at long last, I could.

There was no one in sight as I wove my way among the gravestones. The peace of the graveyard was welcome after the exhausting week I had just endured. Finally, in a corner, I found the stone I was searching for:

Jonathan Sinclair

Kneeling down and pulling my glove off, I ran my hand over the cold stone. "Oh, Jonathan." Deep in my heart, I knew that a woman would never have been entrusted the kind of secrets he'd carried with him. Still, I wished there had been some way he could have told me what he was doing for our country.

Our parents, or at least our father, had known the task Jonathan had taken on. I had been left to believe my brother merely traveled for pleasure. I couldn't help but feel I hadn't known my brother at the end of his life. Tears welled up in my eyes, and I took a deep breath, trying to push away the grief.

My gaze shifted to the small bouquet of violets, limp and half dead already, that rested against the base of the gravestone. Startled, I realized then that my brother's grave appeared to have been looked after diligently in the last five years.

Who would have done such a kind thing? A friend of Jonathan's?

Shaking my head, I found a small grave with grass grown up around it and sat on the gravestone. There was yet another purpose for my long walk. Sure of being unseen by anyone who might carry tales, I pulled a letter from my reticule. It was thicker than usual, which meant my great-aunt had forwarded my correspondence. Since it was not usual for me to receive many letters, this was a surprise.

My Aunt Beth's letter was the first one I read, and amid her Shakespearean insults that I had little patience to decipher, it detailed her disappointment in me. She wondered how I could persist in the pretense of being a lady's maid, asked when I would be returning, and informed me I had missed Mr. Henry Bladen's visit. He had, fortunately, accepted her excuse of my being indisposed and had not returned.

The only word that came to mind when I read those words was, good. What kind of fickle woman did he imagine me to be? He was the one who had abandoned me when I had needed him and then had remained absent for five years. If he believed he could reappear and my affections would be unchanged, he was mistaken.

As they invariably did, as of late, when it came to affection, my thoughts turned to Mr. Oswyn Harper. Had he tried to discover my whereabouts? Not that he had any reason to do so, as I had stumbled upon his traitor for him. Why would he think of me again?

With a shake of my head and mentally scolding myself for being a fool, I folded Aunt Beth's letter and turned my attention to the letter she had enclosed. I didn't immediately recognize the handwriting, but when I opened it and read the salutation I knew. There was only one person who ever referred to me as 'Jules,' and that was my longtime friend, Mary Thornton, nee Heath.

With a sigh, I scanned through most of her barely legible writing. Her correspondence was exactly like her personality: erratic and bubbly. She had been married for four years, and her habit of letter writing had tapered off to an occasional, random missive.

'How laughable to think that I have been married so long and have children of my own. I do wish you could be as happily settled as I am, Jules. Perhaps you should come for a visit, and I can introduce you to all of my neighbors. There are several eligible young men who would be worthy of you...'

Sighing, I broke off my perusal of Mary's letter. She'd written similar sentiments many times over the years, and I had never taken her up on her offer. At first, Henry Bladen had been a shadow on my heart, but now? Now I didn't feel like I knew myself at all, and if I didn't know myself, how could I expect someone else to come to know me?

I glanced one last time at my brother's grave. "I will find out what happened to you, Jonathan," I promised. "And, if I possibly can, I'll make sure justice is done and the traitor is found."

The last would be an almost impossible task, and I knew it. Still, it seemed like something I needed to say, a promise I had to make. It would give me the patience to get me through the long days.

FEELING MORE AT PEACE with myself and my goals, I re-entered Bath. I was halfway to the Dunbar home when someone crashed into my back. As I stumbled, my grip tightened on my reticule, as I knew well the tricks of a boy on the street. It was fortunate that I did so for I felt a firm tug on my purse, but I managed to keep it in my hand. When I had regained my balance, I spotted a child dressed in tatters racing away.

"Pardon me, miss," a male voice called, behind me. "Are you uninjured?"

Turning, I took in the young man. He didn't appear to be very much older than me. "No harm was done," I said, patting my reticule. "Thank you for your concern."

He gave a small chuckle. "I am glad to hear it. It seems to be only I who have suffered a loss to the scamp."

"Perhaps he believed he had more need of it than you," I said, unable to keep a smile from my lips. The child vanished from sight, and the man did not give chase or call out as I had expected him to.

Pale gray eyes flicked over me, and interest sparked on the man's face. "I don't believe we have been introduced."

His tone was curious; otherwise, his words could have been understood a direct cut. Oddly enough, this triggered my amusement, and I bite off a laugh. "Indeed, I would be astonished if we had, sir."

"And why would you say that?"

My amusement faded as I steeled myself to be honest. On the surface, this light-hearted young man seemed to be one I would have readily enjoyed passing my time with if I had been a young lady visiting Bath like any other. However, lamenting what could not be was hardly a productive use of my faculties. "Because I am Miss Dunbar's maid."

His eyebrows went up in surprise, but he didn't walk away. "I am Adam Melbourne," he said to my surprise. "I am an acquaintance of Miss Dunbar and her family. I ought to have guessed a new maid had been employed as Miss Dunbar has been in fine looks as of late. May I know the name of her miracle worker?"

"Miss Julie Nelson." The name rolled off my tongue so easily. It almost felt more comfortable than 'Juliet Sinclair.' "It was a pleasure to meet you, sir."

"May I have the honor of escorting you? After all, a young ruffian may decide your reticule worth his time."

Surprised by the offer, I studied him for a moment. Mr. Melbourne was dressed in the impeccable garb of a young gentleman —tan breeches, a dark blue coat, and black topper. He was slightly taller than me, his build solid. Appearances could be deceiving, though, for all he looked to be respectable and relatively harmless.

"I promise I won't bite." He said this with a smile as if to put me at ease.

Deciding to take the chance, I inclined my head in acceptance and began walking. He fell in step beside me, and we went several minutes without saying anything. "Perhaps you could help me with a bit of a puzzle," he finally said. "I must confess I have an interest in your mistress, Miss Dunbar."

Of course he did. Why else would he still be walking and talking with a maid? "You do get to the point quickly," was all I said.

"She is the most beautiful girl I have ever seen," he continued, his tone fervid and admiring. I barely kept from rolling my eyes. "An incomparable if ever a person deserved to be called such."

Rose Dunbar was, without a doubt, a beautiful young lady. Golden hair and bright blue eyes gave her an angelic appearance. She was petite and knew how to speak with softness. If an elderly lady were present at a gathering, Miss Dunbar would offer her arm or beg to be of some assistance. I had heard many sing her praises during my time in Bath.

However, that was the face she presented to the members of society. In private, she was the most self-centered, spoiled girl I had ever had the misfortune to come across.

"You wish to be in her good graces, then, Mr. Melbourne?" I had wondered how long it would take before a gentleman thought to use me as a way to get inside information concerning Miss Dunbar. A mere two weeks, apparently.

"I will not ask you to do anything unethical. I simply wish to know her likes and dislikes. Anything that will give me an advantage among her admirers."

Feeling a wave of sadness, I shook my head. Mr. Melbourne seemed to be sincere and, at least on the surface, a good man.

Rose Dunbar would use him, flirt with him, and then leave him for the first rogue that caught her eye.

"She has a fondness for roses," I said with a sigh. Even if I told him all I knew about my employer, he wouldn't believe me. He would have to discover the truth of Miss Dunbar's character for himself.

"I could have guessed that."

Anxious to end the conversation, I quickened my steps. "She is also fond of novels. She is as accomplished as any other young lady. That is all I can tell you, Mr. Melbourne. I have not been with Miss Dunbar long enough to have a better grasp on what she does or does not enjoy."

Quickly, Mr. Melbourne matched my gait. "Never say Miss Dunbar is a novel reader!"

"I believe I just did," I said irritably. Miss Dunbar had often in the past two weeks sent me to the bookshop to search out a gothic novel, or some poetry, and she kept Mrs. Radcliffe's novels next to her bed.

"Have I offended you in some way?"

Forcing my annoyance away, I shook my head. "Indeed not, sir."

"I find I don't quite believe you."

"What you choose to believe, sir, is entirely up to you." Primness had crept into my voice, and I cringed at how like a strict governess I sounded. "I am not certain knowing these details will give you an advantage with Miss Dunbar."

Mr. Melbourne heaved a sigh. "No doubt you are right. She is unconcerned with such material things."

Remembering Miss Dunbar's disdain at buying anything when the shopkeeper had a sale, I bit my lip and stared straight ahead. The idea of moderation in spending was foreign to her. She would rather be able to brag about how much she spent on a bit of lace with the notion that the more expensive, the better.

"Unless you want to give her the idea that you desire a relationship with her maid, I suggest you leave me here," I told him, as we drew closer to the Dunbar home on Milsom St. "It would hardly be encouragement for her to show interest in your suit if she were to see me walking with you."

Though, I had the suspicion that it would inspire jealousy from Miss Dunbar and to be caught in such a situation would have been highly uncomfortable. As it was, I had no inclination to encourage a match between my mistress and Mr. Melbourne. He did not deserve a wife such as Miss Dunbar would make.

With a dramatic sigh, Mr. Melbourne took my hand and bowed over it before I could object. "I am not deterred," he said, straightening with a smile. "Good day, Miss Nelson."

With quick strides, he continued on his way and strode past the Dunbar residence as though he had no notion the object of his adoration resided within. With a shake of my head, I made my way to the servants' entrance.

I could only hope the man had his eyes opened before he made a grave mistake.

Eugenia

(A Sinclair Society Novella)

IT IS EUGENIA BURNHAM'S first season, and nothing is going right. Her hair is unmanageable and no lady's maid seems capable of remaining more than a week at a time. Her mother has high expectations of her marrying well and pushes her forward on every opportunity.

Mr. Gerard Landon has been kind to her, but Eugenia doubts she will be able to keep his attention with so many other lovely young ladies in town. With the arrival of a strange new lady's maid, Julie Nelson, she begins to hope that she might have her happy ending after all.

Eugenia is a parallel novella to Regency Rumors, Book One of The Sinclair Society series and is available in ebook format.

Acknowledgments

THIS BOOK WOULD NOT be what it is today without the help of a few other people. A huge thank you to Carissa Dillon for editing and polishing up my book better than I'd ever hoped for. Thank you to my sister for being my first reader, and my mom for being my first critic. I'm thankful to my writer's group for always supporting me. And, of course, I can't forget about my lovely followers on Wattpad for being with me from the beginning.

You all rock!

Also Available By Bethany Swafford

A Chaotic CourtshipA Gentleman of Misfortune: Not My Idea

The Cousin Trilogy:

EMILY'S CHOICE
    Lady Evan Wins the Day

The Sinclair Society series:
Regency Rumors
Eugenia (A Sincalir Society Novella)
The Debutante
Grace (A Sinclair Society Novella)
Clarendon Estate

Young Adult Historical Fiction:

MY HANDS HOLD MY STORY

About the Author

For as long as she can remember, Bethany Swafford has loved reading books. That love of words extended to writing as she grew older and when it became more difficult to find a 'clean' book, she determined to write her own. Among her favorite authors are Jane Austen, Sir Arthur Conan Doyle, and Georgette Heyer. When she doesn't have a pen to paper (or fingertips to a laptop keyboard), she can be found with a book in hand.

To get notified about new releases and any news, sign up to Bethany's Newsletter here: https://bit.ly/2Hg7KJw

Read more at https://bethanyswaffordauthor.wordpress.com/.

www.ingramcontent.com/pod-product-compliance
Lightning Source LLC
LaVergne TN
LVHW041627060526
838200LV00040B/1477